40 and Flashing (the Scotsman)

SILVER FOXES OF BLACK WOLF'S BLUFF

BOOK FOUR

ELLA SHERIDAN

Praise for Silver Foxes of Black Wolf's Bluff

"[A] fascinating series."

WENDY'S BOOK BLOG

"Fun, easy to read, and the start of what seems to be a dynamite series."

THE ORIGINAL MRS. P

"Loved the town and omg that passion between JD and Lily burned the pages!!! Amazing book!"

CK BOOKSTAMMER

"Where sexual tension and drama really heats up in the kitchen."

THE DRAGON DEN BOOK BLOG

"Going back to Black Wolf's Bluff … was such a delight."

GERI'S BOOKISH LIFE

Also by Ella Sheridan

If Only

Only for the Weekend

Only for the Night

Only for the Moment

Only If You Stay

Secrets

Unavailable

Undisclosed

Unshakable

∞

For news on Ella's new releases, free book opportunities, and more, sign up for her VIP Reader List at ellasheridanauthor. com .

Join Ella's Escape Room on Facebook for daily fun, games, and first dibs on all the news!

Silver Foxes of Black Wolf's Bluff: 40 and Flashing (the Scotsman)

Copyright © 2023 Ella Sheridan

Cover Design: Sweet 'n' Spicy Designs

Photographer: Furious Fotog

Cover Model: Joey Berry

Published in the United States

CHAPTER

One

"**F**or someone who flies all the time, you sure hate planes with a passion," Carter said.

Gavin Blackwood frowned at his best friend and business partner. "Nog planes. Seats. It's the fuc"—he caught himself with a glance down at Carter's wide-eyed son, Thad —"er…seats." He shook out his aching legs as the three made their way down the concourse toward what would hopefully be an acceptable breakfast. Airport food was almost as minging as airplane seats.

Okay, call him a snob. He preferred the term *particular,* but whatever. He spent most of his life traveling, so it seemed counterproductive to also spend it denying that he enjoyed the simple pleasures in life. Multiple times he'd considered learning to fly himself or hiring a private plane, but why add to the greenhouse emissions for himself when he could spread the burden across a full flight?

"Was business class not comfortable for some reason?" his friend asked, guiding Thad into the line waiting outside the restaurant.

"I didn't end up in business class." And coach fucking sucked. There, he could say it in his head without corrupting young minds. Travel brought out the grump in him when not much else did. What he didn't tell Carter was that he'd given up his business-class seat to a young mother with a crying babe halfway through the eight-hour flight. Long legs or no, he hadn't been able to stand the wee one's pitiful cries when he could provide a small amount of comfort.

The hostess found them a table, and the cheerful chatter of happy travelers wrapped around him as Carter and Thad settled on food. The holiday decorations and the joy of people on the way to their Christmas celebrations helped lift his mood, as did the cocktail he ordered with his breakfast. It might be ten a.m. in New York, but it had been noon when he left Scotland eight hours ago. That made it time for drinking back home despite the eggs and rashers on his plate. Carter and his son had arrived at the airport early for their flight in order to share a meal before the three of them took the next leg from New York to Nashville. Then it was a four-hour slog of a drive from Nashville to Black Wolf's Bluff, where they should arrive right on time for JD and Lily's rehearsal dinner tonight.

The thought of his friends' Christmas Day wedding lifted his spirits even more. December was his favorite time of the year despite what was usually wet, gloomy Edinburgh weather, perhaps because he received a perverse delight out of loving something his father hated. Having lived around the bah-humbug attitude of his da all his life, he'd thrown himself into the Christmas spirit from a young age. He couldn't think of a better time of year for a wedding, particularly in the lovely Tennessee mountains. They were even predicting snow.

The next leg of the journey felt twice as long despite taking half the time. Carter urged him to catch some z's, but dealing with jet lag frequently had taught him to keep himself awake as long as possible for the early hours of the day in whatever location he found himself. When they landed in Nashville, Carter drove the SUV east toward the small town that JD had grown up in, so Gavin allowed himself a short nap in the car to get him through the evening's festivities. By the time they exited the interstate and passed a McDonald's Thad informed him was the landmark that meant they were "almost there," he was awake and ready to be out of a moving vehicle of any kind for a good long time.

On a long stretch of winding road strangely reminiscent of rural Scotland, bare of any landmarks, Carter slowed and made a left turn that took them up a mountainside. Fresh pavement formed a three-lane road Carter informed him had been put in place in October when he and Thad first visited. In the back seat, Carter's son was bouncing within the confines of his seat belt as they made their way up. The altitude put pressure on Gavin's ears much like the airplane rides had. About halfway up the mountain, a stone fence appeared alongside the road, leading to stone pillars holding an open gate. Through the entrance was a large manor house, its wings spread to either side in a wide vee.

JD Lane stepped onto the small portico as they drove into the courtyard. His friend's tall frame fit with the elaborate home his family had built years ago. Coming back to this town and this house had not been easy for the man, but he'd found a happiness none of them expected when he'd met the mayor of Black Wolf's Bluff, Lily Easton. Now the two would be married in a few short days.

JD jogged out to welcome them as Carter parked the SUV. "Hey!" He snatched Thad up for a hug when the ten-year-old tried to zoom past him. "What's your hurry?"

Thad laughed, squirming in his "uncle's" hold. "I want to see Erin."

"Well, give me a hug first."

After JD squeezed a hug out of him, the boy sprinted uphill to find Erin, Carter's girlfriend—although Gavin

3

suspected the relationship was more serious than the term *girlfriend* signified.

"Don't go up that mountain in the dark without me," Carter called.

"Aw, Dad!"

Carter gave his son a stern look. "You can wait two minutes."

And two minutes was all it took for Carter to unpack the SUV and turn to follow his son up the hill.

"Abandonin' me so soon, brother?" Gavin asked his departing back.

Carter turned around but kept walking backward, a grin lighting up his face. "No offense, but you aren't as good-looking as Erin."

"What? I don' believe that."

"Believe it."

"Dad!"

"Duty calls," Carter said to Gavin. His face held no hint of regret.

"I don' think it's duty so much as"—he looked past Carter to Thad and his wee listening ears and held back the word on the tip of his tongue—"somethin' else."

"You know it." Carter gave him a sarcastic salute. "Bye."

Gavin chuckled as he hauled his carry-on inside.

"Ya've completed a lot more of the renovations than I realized," he observed as JD showed him to a room.

"The manor should be complete by February. No thanks to Linc throwing us off schedule."

"Oh?"

"Carter didn't tell you that story?" JD chuckled. "Linc decided on his first visit to preempt Erin's construction plans and start on the complete gutting of the kitchen so he would have an excuse to horn his way into Claire's bakery."

Gavin grinned. "Sounds like that twat."

The kitchen was spectacular; Gavin had to give Linc that

much credit. Chrome and stainless steel sparkled in the bright overhead lights as he and JD entered after stowing his things upstairs. Lily, JD's fiancée, sat at the bar countertop, a glass of what he presumed was sweet tea—given that they were in the South—condensating at her elbow.

Gavin held out his arms. "Lily, love!"

"Gavin!"

They hadn't met face-to-face before now, but he and Lily had spoken via chat and video calls with JD several times. The bride-to-be stood to give him a welcome hug. Gavin threw in a quick kiss on the cheek just to hear JD complain. Lily's amused look said she knew his game well. He imagined Linc played the same one—JD was nothing if not predictable.

Settled at the bar with a hot tea, also sweet, he and Lily chatted about wedding details for a while, JD joining in between work phone calls.

"No one wants to lose the chance to talk to him before he goes offline," Lily explained.

"And when is that?" Gavin asked.

"Right now," JD said, clicking his phone off. He walked around the island to give his fiancée a quick kiss. "No more work till we get back from the honeymoon. My new admin is more than capable of handling anything else."

"With Christmas four days away, everyone else will be going offline soon too." Lily lifted her glass and sipped her tea, humming as the cool liquid hit her tongue.

JD cleared his throat, shifting behind the island. Gavin hid a smile. Good to know the sparks were alive and well for his friends.

Lily, seeming oblivious to her effect on her fiancé, glanced at her watch. "I need to get ready so I can swing by and pick up Scarlett on our way to the restaurant."

Gavin paused, teacup halfway to his mouth. "Anythin' I can help with?"

"Oh, no, I couldn't ask."

Gavin gave her his flirtiest grin. "Put me to work, please."

JD grunted his displeasure. "Yes, Lily, put him to work."

Gavin winked at Lily from the side JD couldn't see.

Lily chuckled but shook her head. "My friend Scarlett needs a ride to the rehearsal dinner, but navigating these hills can be a PITA." She shot JD a frown. "I wouldn't ask someone who's never been here to drive them at night."

Gavin scoffed. "Have ya no' seen roads in Scotland? One lane and two cars, my bonnie lass." He laid the brogue on thick.

"Let him go, Lily," JD said. "Maybe he'll get lost and we won't have to put up with his flirting all night at the rehearsal dinner."

Lily gave her fiancé a look.

JD gave her an insincere smile in return. "No, seriously, please send him. He can practice his playboy act on your single friends instead of you."

Gavin's ears perked up. "Single friends?"

Lily's eyes sparkled. "That got your attention, huh?"

"It did." He splayed a dramatic hand over his heart. "Did Carter not tell ya why I came to Black Wolf's Bluff?"

"For our wedding?" JD interjected.

Gavin rolled his eyes. "O' course not." He turned his attention back to Lily. "Every time one of my friends comes here to visit, they find their dream woman. Why should I be any different?" Not that he was looking for a dream woman, if one even existed for him. His father, on the other hand, had been married six times. Gavin had put strict boundaries around his own love life for that very reason, long ago. But he wasn't above a good time while he was here.

After a moment of thought, Lily gave in. "I should probably be offended by the fact that our wedding isn't a priority—"

"Now, I never said that."

"You didn't *not* say it either," Lily pointed out, her amusement plain. "So I'll give you the directions, but no funny business with my friend, got it, Gavin? I don't want any heartbreak after my wedding when you fly back off to Edinburgh."

"Sure now, Lily. This charm is a weapon that must be wielded with care. I promise to leave all the female residents of Black Wolf's Bluff with whole hearts."

"You'd better." After giving him directions as well as the address for his GPS, Lily sent him down the mountain toward town in JD's SUV.

CHAPTER
Two

"Damn, damn, damn." Scarlett whipped her towel off over her wet head and fanned herself with it. "Damn these hot flashes!" Perimenopause should come with warning signs the size of bulletin boards. And an opt-out option would be nice too. All it took was one wrong move—bending to get something from a drawer, walking inside from the cool outside, getting out of the shower—and great balls of fire ignited in her body, sucking every bit of coolness out and replacing it with a pulsating heat that felt like it would never end. She never knew when one would strike, never knew if the next moment would be the one where she'd pray to be hosed down with ice to get rid of the internal inferno.

It really wasn't fair. Men didn't go through a phase of life where they got out of the shower sweating. Where they had to run a full-on fan in order to keep their skin color normal and not mimicking a lobster fresh out of a boiling pot of water. Why? Why why why was midlife like this for women?

She grabbed her robe from the hook behind the bathroom door and tugged it onto each arm as she sped down the hall to the kitchen. The rush of frigid air when she opened the freezer door felt like heaven, chilling her bare skin immediately. How long she stood there, soaking in the cold, she had no idea, but however long it took, she'd stay. Anything to get her temperature out of the fever zone.

It didn't help that she really needed to hurry. In fact, she found it only made the hot flashes worse if she was rushing around. Which made getting ready to go somewhere the primary time these damn episodes hit. Instead of getting her clothes on, she was taking them off in a desperate attempt to cool down. She raised her chin, sighing as frosty air washed over her neck and chest. Lord, it felt almost as good as an orgasm, not that she'd had one of those in a while. There weren't a lot of dating options in Black Wolf's Bluff. When she'd moved here a year ago, looking for a place away from big-city Nashville that she could settle into and build a home that would suit her lifestyle, she hadn't factored in the lack of local single men, especially in her age range. And every new man that showed up had immediately paired with one of her single friends. If anything, it felt like her libido was withering on a vine with no one to pluck it.

A giggle escaped at the terrible analogy. She was a romance writer, for goodness' sake. Couldn't she do better than that?

A knock at the front door signaled Lily's arrival. Scarlett hated to ask her friend for a ride to the rehearsal dinner, but Lily lived just up the street, and Scarlett's car had been in the shop all week. Though Robert was a great mechanic, he was anything but fast. And like her dating options, good mechanics were hard to come by in a small town like Black Wolf's Bluff.

Refusing to move away from the chilled air caressing her skin, she yelled over her shoulder, "Come in!"

The front door opened. "I'm in the kitchen," she called and leaned her forehead against the freezer door, relieved at feeling the heat in her body finally starting to ease. She flapped the sides of her robe a couple of times, encouraging the air flow, waiting for Lily to come down the hall. "I just need a few minutes to finish getting ready. Sorry I'm running late."

"I don' mind waitin'."

Every cell in her body froze. That voice wasn't Lily's. In fact, it was a couple of octaves below her friend's light and cheerful voice. Definitely masculine—and definitely unfamiliar.

Without thought, she jerked around to face the stranger who had entered her kitchen. "Who are you?"

Standing in the doorway was a tall, dark-haired man she'd never met before. Salt-and-pepper curls dangled over his forehead, adding to the mischievous look in his pretty amber eyes. Stubble graced his squared-off jaw and framed a full mouth that quirked to one side.

"I'm Gavin." That whisky-colored gaze ran down her body, appreciation lighting it up. "Ya must be Scarlett. Nice to meet ya."

She hadn't realized until she felt the touch of that look that she was standing, open freezer at her back, with the lapels of her robe in each hand.

Her open robe. That was supposed to be covering her naked body.

And wasn't.

Holy shit.

She rapidly clutched the sides of her robe together over her chest. "I'm so sorry. I— I—"

His grin was the sexiest thing she'd seen in a very long while. "Don' apologize. I was enjoying the view."

Her hot flash might have ended, but she was heating up for a whole different reason now. Embarrassment. "Oh my God. I'm so—" She gulped.

He winked. "Ya definitely are, lass."

Lass? Did he call her *lass*? "Okay, first of all, a lass is young, which I most definitely am not…"

He chuckled. "Younger than me, I'm pretty sure. And sweet to boot."

Sweet? "Who are you again?"

He stepped forward, hand out. "Gavin Blackwood. I came to give ya a lift to the rehearsal dinner."

She instinctively shook. Gavin. Gavin… "Carter's business partner, right?"

"Indeed."

The Scotsman. Gavin was Scottish, and now that she thought about it, she could detect the hint of brogue in his words. The knowledge sent heat toward her middle. She'd always wanted to meet a man with a Scottish accent, and despite Gavin's being faint, he definitely qualified. Not to mention he was sexy as all get out.

And he was still holding her hand. Clutching her robe like a damsel afraid of being ravaged, she pulled her hand from his grip. He seemed reluctant to let go.

"Where is Lily?"

"She was up the mountain, so I offered to help."

She could've given me a heads-up. Although she might have; Scarlett couldn't remember where she'd set her phone, a not uncommon occurrence for her. Her head tended to be in a story, not so much in reality.

"Okay, well…" She felt like she was tripping over her tongue. It wasn't every day a total stranger saw you naked, not to mention one that looked like Gavin. Considering her luck, however, he'd meet another of her single friends at the wedding and fall desperately in love. Best not to get attached.

Her gaze drifted down his body. She was probably already getting too attached. Broad shoulders, thick chest, solid all the way down. She'd never gone for the swimmer's body—give her a man's solid weight against her any day and she'd be a happy woman.

"Well…?"

Gavin's voice brought her back to reality. Right. "Uh, just let me finish dressing—"

"Don' hurry on my account."

Her cheeks heated. Keep this up and she'd start another hot flash any minute. She ducked her head. "I'll be right back. Make yourself comfortable?"

She didn't wait for his answer, simply darted around him and shot down the hall as fast as her bare feet would take her. The masculine chuckle that followed her did nothing to ease her blush, so the second she got the bathroom door closed, she jerked the cold water on, held a washcloth under it, and brought it to the back of her neck.

Aaah! Blessed relief.

She did her best not to rush as she finished getting dressed and put on makeup. The thick curls falling down her back were mostly dry by the time she finished, so she hit them with the hair dryer for a couple of minutes and was done. Stepping into her bedroom, she listened carefully but didn't hear any sound from Gavin, so she shut the door and eyed herself in the full-length mirror on the back as she added some simple gold hoops to her ears. The temperature outside had been dropping all day, putting it close to freezing tonight. She wore thick leggings tucked into her favorite knee-high boots, and a long sweater that reached her thighs and cinched just below her breasts. The dark green color brought out her eyes, she thought, and made her feel pretty with the ruffles lining the deep vee of the top.

Would Gavin like the color?

Oh, for fuck's sake, stop thinking about Gavin!

Hard to do when the man had seen her naked. When she could physically feel the touch of his gaze over her body even in her memories. Her nipples felt sensitive just thinking about it. How was she supposed to stop?

Better figure out a way, Scarlett. You write romance; you know meet-cutes like that don't happen in real life.

Well, they did happen—he had definitely walked into her kitchen and seen her naked—but they didn't lead to lifelong love. Some women ended up alone. She'd accepted that fate a long time ago, but it didn't mean a little romance was unwanted. And who wouldn't fantasize about the sexy Scotsman? There'd probably be plenty of women, of all ages, with their tongues hanging out when he walked through the door tonight.

When she entered the living room, Gavin was standing at her floor-to-ceiling bookshelves that lined the far wall, perusing the titles. Was he a reader? Somehow she could picture him with a glass of whisky in one hand, a cigar resting at his elbow on a side table, a roaring fire crackling nearby, but she wasn't certain she could see a book in his empty hand.

She cleared her throat. "I'm ready."

Gavin swung around, his gaze trailing her body just as it had before. "Gorgeous. The green is bonnie good on ya."

Damn blushes. She never knew what to say to compliments like that. "Thank you."

He jerked a thumb over his shoulder. "Avid reader?"

"I'm an author, actually."

His eyes widened, sparkling with what looked like pleasure. "Are ya now? What do ya write?"

She moved to collect her purse and coat from the coat rack next to the door. "Romance."

"Ah. Seems apt."

She eyed him as she put on her coat, but there was no mocking in his expression. That was the reaction that she received most when people—especially single men—found out what she wrote. Score one for Gavin, though if she was honest with herself, he'd scored about a hundred since he'd arrived. She had a feeling he was a flirt of the highest caliber.

"A couple of my stepsisters are romance readers. JR Ward,

Nora Roberts. Got me hooked on Lisa Gardner—she's a good one with a mystery."

Lisa Gardner was one of her favorites too. When she was actively writing, she didn't read contemporary romance, so she'd found favorites in other genres as well. "Do you read thrillers mostly?"

"Eh, a bit of everythin'." He waved toward the horror section of her shelves. "Jonathan Maberry is another one I'm keen on. Love his Joe Ledger series."

Another good choice. She was impressed. "*Patient Zero* is phenomenal. And when I don't want to read romance, his zombie novels are always fun."

Gavin chuckled. "Always." He tilted his head as he considered her. "Do ya use a pseudonym?"

"Oh, definitely." She picked up her purse. Thankfully none of her own books were out here; she kept them on the shelves in her office. Anytime someone she'd been interested in had tried to read one of her books, the results had been disastrous. Men couldn't seem to understand that just because you wrote about it didn't necessarily mean you wanted to live it out. The number of men who'd turned into assholes because they'd skimmed an antihero book of hers, not to mention the ones who thought she must be a nympho-maniac because her books contained sex, had taught her well to keep her pen name under wraps.

Gavin crossed the room toward her. "Not gonna share, eh?"

"No way."

She noticed again that his grin had a lopsided quality that gave him a boyish look. She couldn't drag her eyes away when that grin appeared on his face. "I'll have to ask someone else then."

He probably would, but she really hoped he wouldn't. She'd have to pass the word to her girlfriends not to share. But then again, Gavin would be gone in a few short days. She probably wouldn't see him after tonight until the wedding, and then he'd be back to Scotland or New York or wherever, and she'd be back to her quiet life in the country with no Scotsman to talk to.

Better to not get attached, right?

CHAPTER
Three

S carlett walked ahead of him to the waiting SUV. The thick coat kept her warm against the chill air, but he cursed its bulkiness as it hid the sway of her generous hips and sexy legs in those lovely leather boots. He'd always adored a woman in boots. Lily had warned him off her friend, but she hadn't warned him of how sexy Scarlett was. And now that he knew what was beneath all those layers…

She was lovely, indeed; a sight he wouldn't be forgetting anytime soon, for certain.

He handed her into the car, then rounded the back to climb into the driver's seat. The first thing he noticed was her scent—warm vanilla and sugar. Perfect for eating.

Get yer mind off the lass, Gav. Ye're not here for romancin'.

That didn't mean he couldn't, though, did it?

He breathed in her heady scent as he put the SUV into reverse. "Can ya direct me to the restaurant?"

"Of course." That pretty smile took over her lips, and when he looked her way, he could see a faint blush on her cheeks despite the winter darkness outside. That blush made him want to take her clothes off, find out exactly how far he could get it to spread.

He forced his gaze back to the road.

Companionable silence took over as she gave him instructions through town. When they were on the road to Gatlinburg, he engaged her with a bit of chatter about the wedding, trying to draw her out. From the bit Carter had told him about Lily's friends, Scarlett was the one who kept mostly quiet unless she had something to say. Gavin found he enjoyed the sound of her voice, the way her words tended to take on a whimsy that showed her creative side. Even discussing the restaurant they were headed to, The Carousel, she painted a picture in his mind with very little effort. He liked that about her.

He liked her, and not only looking at her.

The Carousel was not far off Main Street in Gatlinburg, lit up with bright lights shining in the darkness where it perched on an ledge overlooking a lake. Gavin had traveled the world, and he had to admit he'd seen few sights as pretty as the glass-sided restaurant glowing in the night. The lot was crowded, but he found a spot close to the door for them.

When he shut the SUV off, Scarlett reached for the door handle.

"No, wait," he said. "I'll come around."

Scarlett seemed surprised but waited as he rounded the back end of the SUV and opened her door with a flourish. Offering her his hand, he smiled. "Ready to have some fun?"

She gave him a rueful look. "I hope you have plenty of energy after flying all day. JD is big on dancing."

She didn't have to tell him. The man's obsession had started in college when he became the official DJ for their fraternity parties. He'd taught himself to dance, guaranteeing that he was never without a date. "JD always did love a dance."

Her smile was both sweet and seductive, especially with the red lipstick she'd put on in the car. It made him want to wear some of that lipstick—in inappropriate places, of course.

He really was captivated with the wee kitten, wasn't he?

Taking Scarlett's hand, he threaded it through his arm to escort her inside.

The party had the restaurant to themselves for the night. Walking inside, they were met with a wall of noise—people talking, laughing, even some singing. Gavin soaked in the atmosphere, feeling his energy rise as only a true extrovert could do. Scarlett, on the other hand, handed over her coat but seemed hesitant to join the crowd.

Gavin bent to her ear. "Do ya know everyone here?"

She turned to him, the move bringing their faces close together. "The people from town, at least. JD has a lot of clients here from out of town." She tucked her hair behind her ear. "I think they also invited anyone who wasn't able to come on Christmas Day, so it's not your typical rehearsal dinner. More like a pre-wedding party."

That explained it. "Would ya be willing to introduce me around?" It was a way to keep her near him, aye, but he wasn't going to apologize for that. He was often pegged as a playboy when what he really was, was a man who enjoyed pleasure. If being near a woman gave him pleasure, he stayed. As long as he kept to his rule of no more than a week together, he was fine.

Why a week? It probably sounded ridiculous—why put an arbitrary limit on the amount of time he could spend with a woman? And of course, like all things ridiculous in adulthood, it stemmed from his childhood experiences with his father. William Blackwood had rarely met a woman he didn't want. Unfortunately he too often mistook lust for love—the man had married six times already. And in every instance he'd spent mere days with the woman before rushing off to elope.

Gavin wouldn't put himself or a woman through that kind of roller coaster. So he stuck to his rule, ridiculous or not.

Scarlett glanced behind him, then shook her head. "I think Carter has other plans."

He followed her look to see his friend headed their way. He gave Scarlett's hand a squeeze. "Save me a dance then?"

She hesitated, then nodded. "I will."

"I'll find ya later."

He watched Scarlett join a small group of women her age, including Erin, Carter's fiancée, whom he'd met before. One of the women had to be in her eighties, and his eyes shot wide when he noticed that she had a leash in her hand. At the other end was a huge tomcat, daintily cleaning its paw as it watched the crowd around it.

A cat at a rehearsal dinner. That was definitely a new one on him.

Carter stopped beside him and snagged flutes of champagne off a passing waiter's tray for each of them. "Thanks."

The waiter nodded. "Dinner will be out shortly."

Carter handed Gavin a glass. "You didn't get lost in the woods."

He scoffed. "Me? Are ya off yer head?"

Carter laughed. "Considering how many times you've almost gotten me killed driving in Scotland, I had no doubt you'd be back in one piece."

Gavin sipped the champagne while arching a superior brow at his friend. Carter slapped him on the back. "Let me show you around."

Thus began the whirlwind of introductions to what seemed like every person who must live in this tiny town. He met members of the town council, Lily's admin and his fiancée, her parents, several employees from Claire's bakery, and even Claire. The lovely woman fussed over a cake table, shooing away the Carousel's staff when they would've taken over. "I made the damn thing; I'll take care of it myself."

Carter and Gavin joined a laughing Lincoln at the table.

"You know you're supposed to be off tonight, right, sweet-heart?" Linc was saying.

"I'm never off when my food is nearby."

Lincoln turned to Gavin, reaching to give him a bro hug. "Good to see you." He gestured to Claire. "She really isn't, by the way. It's a fault in her that I can't seem to break."

"Are you saying it's wrong for a woman to care about her job?" Claire asked, glaring down her lover.

Gavin raised his eyebrows. "I don' think I'd answer that one, my friend." He extended his hand. "It's a pleasure to finally meet ya in person, Claire."

"Oh my God, I love your accent." She took his hand.

Gavin added a bit more brogue to his words. "I'm glad it pleases ya, my dear."

Linc forcibly separated their fingers. "If you like it that much, Claire, I'm sure I can figure out how to adopt an accent myself." He glared at Gavin. "Stop flirting with my woman."

"What is it with everyone accusing me of flirtin'?" Gavin grinned. He was flirting, but he also enjoyed giving his friends a hard time.

Linc's glare got harsher. "I know you, Gavin. You'll flirt with anything in a skirt. Or not. Speaking of which, how about I introduce you to our local postmistress."

Turned out the postmistress was the lady with the cat. Snookums. All Gavin could do was shake his head at that. He wasn't sure how successful he was at hiding his surprise from the old dear.

Dinner was excellent, though he'd expected nothing less. Linc gave his best man speech, complete with just the right touch of humor. Claire, as maid of honor, seemed much less polished at speaking in front of a crowd, but no less sincere. It touched Gavin to see how the friendships between his friends had flourished for the past thirty years. Carter, Lincoln, and JD had met their first year at Columbia. Gavin had shared a class with Carter their junior year and became friends with the men immediately. He and Carter had worked together at an international finance corporation for years before deciding to go out on their own. It was the best decision he'd ever made, businesswise, and his friendship with Carter, Linc, and JD had only grown from there. And now, all these years later, JD was getting married. Gavin had a feeling Lincoln and Carter were not far behind.

His gaze settled on Scarlett, seated next to one of the women he been introduced to earlier—Iris, he believed, the local librarian—and any feelings of loneliness at being surrounded by his attached friends dissipated beneath his attraction to her. The woman made him curious, and curiosity about a woman was definitely something he enjoyed. He simply had to keep it under control. He was here for a week, and he would enjoy spending that week with Scarlett. As long as he took it no further than that, everything would be fine.

All the single ladies had had their dance with Beyoncé by the time Gavin approached Scarlett on the dance floor. Holding out his hand, he said, "This dance is promised to me, I believe."

Cheeks flushed with exertion, Scarlett flushed even deeper, glancing around at her gaping girlfriends before tentatively giving him her hand. "I didn't think you'd remember."

"I never forget a promise," he said, winking over Scarlett's shoulder as her friends giggled. A slow song filtered through the speakers. Anticipation thrummed in his veins as he led Scarlett to an isolated spot on the dance floor and took her into his arms.

She fit perfectly. Somehow he'd known she would despite her five-foot-five-inches or so height. At a couple inches above six feet, he enjoyed a bit of height on a woman, but in her heeled boots, Scarlett was just right.

Hoping to catch her off guard, he led with, "Now what did ya say yer pen name was?"

Scarlett shook her head, tossing him an amused look. "That's not going to work."

"It's not? Damn." He grinned down at her. "Why won't ya tell me? I do want to read one of yer books."

She stared up at him for a few measures, then surprised him by turning serious. "You really want to know?"

He matched her tone. "I really do."

"Okay." She took a deep breath, which pressed her ample breasts into his chest in a way he couldn't ignore. "The truth is, if I wrote mysteries or literature"—she made air quotes with the hand on his arm—"or even horror, I wouldn't hesitate. But men get… strange…when they find out women write romance, particularly open-door romance."

"Open-door?"

"Open bedroom door," she clarified, and when he continued to frown at her, "Explicit."

His cock tightened. He willed it to behave. "Why did they get strange about that? I presume these men are adults who've experienced sex, so…" He arched a brow.

"So they start asking awkward personal questions, like do I practice what I write. Or even worse, assume I do and that makes me available for whatever they want. They don't read my books. They don't appreciate my work. It's just a sex thing to them, and I'm an object, not a human with a brain."

Those men must be twats. If the books contained sex that came from a mind like Scarlett's, he sure as hell wanted to read them. But he wouldn't read only for the sex. "Completin' a book with the intricacies and details to make it popular is beyond my comprehension, Scarlett, so I know for certain ya have a brain, and a damn fine one." He tucked her closer for a turn. "And I don' need to read sex scenes to be interested in ya."

He knew the minute she recognized his hard length

against her soft belly—her eyes went wide, dropping from his, and her blush returned. He was becoming fascinated with that pretty pink color.

"Um…thank you?"

He chuckled. "Ye're more than welcome, lass. Now, what was that pen name?"

CHAPTER
Four

S carlett dreamed about that dance with Gavin and woke hot and bothered in a way she hadn't in years. The dream had progressed from dancing at the Carousel to dancing in other ways, and…

The Scotsman was going to be a problem, wasn't he?

She channeled the energy into her latest sex scene for the book she was writing. Part of a duet, the second installment was the conclusion to a cliffhanger her readers were clamoring for her to finish. Just a few more chapters and she would be done. And in February everyone could stop sending her messages asking what was going to happen. Even her beta readers didn't know.

Thinking about the whole thing made an evil laugh bubble up. Authors didn't talk about it, but most of them enjoyed torturing their readers a little bit. Or a lot. It depended on how sadistic the author was. But all of them had that tendency.

She definitely tended toward the "a lot" end of the spectrum.

She finished her morning writing session around noon and was headed to fix some lunch when a hard knock sounded on her door. Thinking it must be one of her friends with a wedding task they needed help with, she hurried over and opened without checking first.

Gavin stood on the threshold. And from the look on his face, he wasn't happy.

"What—"

"Ya've got ta tell me what happens."

"What happens with what?"

He made an impatient gesture. "Ya know what I mean, Scarlett. What happens with Levi and Abby?"

Shock jolted through her. "Did you read my book?"

"Course I did. Why did ya think I asked for yer pen name?"

Because you were trying to get in my pants? She didn't say that out loud. It sounded way too arrogant. More like something Gavin would say, to be honest. But the thought had occurred to her. He wouldn't be the first to attempt to flatter her by asking. "You read my book." *Okay.* "Already?"

"See," Gavin said, propping a fist high on her doorframe, "the renovated suites have these massive bathtubs."

Oh God, he was doing that book-boyfriend lean that made women go crazy. Eyeing the bicep popping beneath his long-sleeved shirt, she gulped. And what was he saying? What did bathtubs have to do with him—

"Are ya going to invite me in?" He straightened and stomped his feet. "It's a bit chilly out here, and I'm hopin' this conversation takes a while. After ya tell me what happened with the book."

Maybe it was the shock, maybe it was something else, but she found herself stepping back and allowing Gavin into the living room. He shucked his coat and hung it on the coatrack like a gentleman. The thought made her grin. The man appeared to be a gentleman until he opened his mouth—then he was all flirt.

So why had he read her book?

"The bathtubs," he was saying, "are huge, and after bein' cramped up in the airplane all day yesterday, I decided to take a long soak. Unfortunately there was no' a drop o' whisky to accompany me, so I ordered yer book and read it on my phone."

He read her book …on his phone…in the bathtub. In lieu of whisky.

The image flashed in her mind—Gavin naked, the dark hair on his chest wet and dotted with bubbles. One long leg was hooked over the side of the tub, and his long fingers were wrapped around a cut-crystal glass of amber liquid. Head tipped back, a slight smile on his mouth as the hot water caressed his body.

Holy cow.

Focus. Stop thinking about the bath.

So he'd read her book.

"And I couldna stop. I needed to know what happened—except ya cut the damn thing off on a cliffhanger."

Ah, now they got to the crux of the matter. A bubble of glee rose in her chest. "Did that bother you?"

"Did tha'—" A sound much like a growl rumbled through the Scotsman's chest, sending a shiver down her spine. "O' course it bothered me. Ya've got to tell me what happens."

His accent was getting thicker the more agitated he became. "I can't do that."

"Why no'?"

"Because I haven't written it yet."

"Ya haven't written the sequel? It comes out in February."

"I've written some of it. But I don't reveal my plots until the book is completely done."

"Well, ya can reveal it to me!"

"Absolutely not." The glee turned into a wannabe giggle.

"Are ya laughin' at me?"

"No, of course not." Admittedly the words were a bit strangled. That was probably why Gavin glared at her.

"Aye, ya are."

"No, I'm not." She immediately burst into laughter. "Okay, I am."

He paused, his gaze taking her in as she plopped onto the sofa, laughter shaking her whole body.

"It's kind of like giving me a tip," she tried to explain, her words interspersed with gaps filled with amusement. "You buy the book, and that's great because royalties, obviously. But to know that you're so frustrated you came all the way here to find out what happens in the next book? That's the best tip anybody could give an author."

"Ya enjoy my frustration, do ya?"

"I normally wouldn't admit it, but that's because I'm normally hiding behind a keyboard. So yes, I definitely enjoy it."

Gavin began a slow stalk toward the couch. "I may have to extract revenge for that."

"Revenge?" The squeak in her voice embarrassed her.

This time it was Gavin's turn to chuckle. "Revenge."

When he reached the couch, he planted his fists on both sides of her head and leaned over her body. "Aye, lass, I definitely think a bit o' mutual torture is called for."

"Mutual torture?" The words were breathless, anticipation sending her heart into her throat. He was so close she could smell the aftershave he wore, something spicy that tangled in her nose. Exciting, like the man himself. Gavin wasn't like any man she'd ever met—and it wasn't simply because he was Scottish.

"Definitely mutual torture," he murmured, his gaze locking onto her lips.

She licked them.

A flicker crossed his face that she wasn't sure she understood. And then he straightened.

She tried to hold back her whimper but didn't succeed. Gavin gave her a somewhat twisted grin.

Oh. Mutual torture. Ugh.

She tried not to think about the fact that he couldn't be tortured if he wasn't feeling as turned-on as she was. Instead she stood as well. Scrambling for a distraction, she happened on, "Have you had lunch? I was just about to fix some."

He rubbed a hand over his curls. "Might be a better idea if I take ya out to lunch. Know anyplace acceptable?"

"As a matter of fact I do."

Twenty minutes later they were being led to a seat at Casa Blanca, the local Mexican restaurant. Rich, the owner, was a staple in town; he'd grown up with Lily's parents. On their way to the back of the restaurant, he busily quizzed Gavin about his homeland and traveling to the US, which Gavin said he did frequently. Scarlett thought for a few minutes that Rich would never leave their table, but finally he went to grab Gavin's beer and her margarita. Hey, if Gavin was going to drink, she was going to have her favorite too.

"So does that happen all the time?" she asked, her natural curiosity overcoming her tongue-tied-ness around this massively attractive man.

"Does what happen?"

"People quizzing you about Scotland and being Scottish? Americans are fascinated by anything Scots."

"Usually, aye, except this one time with this wee lass in this tiny town in the Tennessee mountains…"

Wee? She was beginning to think the man needed glasses. "Why do you keep calling me 'lass'?"

He arched a brow at her. "Because it suits ya."

"I'm not a young woman," she pointed out.

"And thank God for that." His enthusiasm made her cheeks flush. "When ya say Americans are fascinated by anythin' Scots, that goes double for young women." He chuckled without shame. "It's not often I get to enjoy time with a woman closer to my age. It's nice."

Ignoring the pleasure that filled her at his compliment, she persisted. "So...lass?"

Now he did look slightly embarrassed. "Partly habit," he admitted.

Something like disappointment—but not disappointment; she wasn't disappointed—sank in her chest. "So you don't have to remember the names of the gobs of young females who throw themselves at you?"

"Partly. Women here don't enjoy being called a 'hen.'"

If she'd had a drink, she would have spit it out. "'Hen'?"

"Mmm."

She had to admit she didn't want to be called a *hen* either. Staring back at Gavin, she noticed the amusement looked good on him. Maybe that was why he seemed to prefer that emotion to any other. It took the years off, even as she guess he was slightly older than her, in his late forties or so.

"But did ya know 'lass' doesn't only mean 'young girl,'" he was saying. "It also means 'sweetheart.'"

"So you're using a generic endearment." Was that worse or better?

Did she see color rising in his cheeks? "I'm commentin' on the sweetness I know is you, Scarlett." His amber-colored eyes took on a shine. "I have seen it, after all."

Her cheeks turned hot in an instant. He certainly had.

Rich was busy seating another couple, thank goodness, so Adrian brought their drinks over. He gave Scarlett a wink. "Who's your friend?"

Before she could say, *Carter's friend,* Gavin had his hand out. "Blackwood. Groomsman."

"Oh." The young man shook Gavin's hand with enthusiasm. "Nice to meet you. I'm Adrian. My mom, Maria, runs the coffee shop."

"Now I have heard bonnie things about her coffee."

Adrian's eyes lit up. "She's the best. And her coffee's good too," he teased.

"Maria is the best," Scarlett agreed.

Taking out his order pad, Adrian asked, "What can I get you two to eat?"

They gave their orders and sipped their drinks as they waited for the food to arrive. Watching Gavin gaze around the room, Scarlett couldn't help wondering why the man didn't have anything better to do. So she asked him.

"Don't you have wedding stuff going on? Where are the guys?" *Why are you wasting an afternoon chasing me down about a book ending instead of spending it with your friends?*

He gave her that lopsided grin. "With their fiancées and girlfriends." He laughed. "I knew comin' in that they'd all be occupied. I didn't realize I'd find someone fascinatin' to help me pass the time." He tipped his beer toward her.

She tried hard not to blush. The man made her blush far too much as it was.

"So what is there to do around here besides eat Mexican food and read yer books? Not that I don' want to read more of yer books, but for some reason the author won't tell me what's happenin' next." He gave her what she hoped was a mock glare.

"It's not personal," Scarlett protested.

"On the contrary, it feels very personal." He waggled his brows at her.

"You're a big flirt. You know that, right?"

His eyes went wide. "Me? I have never heard that before, no."

"Liar."

Gavin chuckled. "Al'right, I have heard it before. What can I say? I might be Scottish, but my mam must've kissed the Blarney Stone while she was pregnant with me."

"More like you traveled over to Ireland and kissed it yourself."

His smile said he'd never tell. "So, things to do?"

"At Christmastime there's plenty to do. Black Wolf's Bluff may be small, but they definitely get into the spirit. There's a craft fair with local artists at the community center, cookie decorating at Claire's bakery, hot chocolate at the coffee shop, sleigh rides, Santa visits at various stores, Christmas services at every church in town—of which there are many. This is the South, after all."

He laughed. "We have the same back home, though most of our churches are hundreds of years old."

She'd always dreamed of seeing the castles and churches of Scotland. "I think those are more interesting, at least the buildings." She sipped her drink. "There are also activities in Pigeon Forge and Gatlinburg nearby. Anyway, I'm sure we could find some things for you to occupy yourself with."

"I'd rather ya find some things to occupy *me* with."

She gave him a side-eye.

"Not like that. Though I'm not opposed."

She was sputtering when they were interrupted by the arrival of their food. She kept her skepticism to herself, and by the time Adrian left and the aroma of grilled meat and fresh-made flour tortillas hit her nose, she no longer cared.

"I was thinkin', maybe ya could keep me company this week."

The sinking disappointment in her gut was a surprise. "I appreciate it, Gavin, but I do have to write this week. Despite it being Christmas, I need to get the last few chapters finished. You want the next book, don't you?"

He glared. "Ye're goin' to keep that danglin' over my head, aren't ya?"

She gave him a sweet smile.

"Fine." He took a bite of fajita meat and chewed slowly. After swallowing, he took a swallow of beer, and she couldn't help but think that he was scheming behind those too-gorgeous eyes.

"How about this?" He reached across the table to grasp

her hand. "Ya keep me company part of the day, and I can keep ya company while ya write."

"I don't have company while I write."

He rolled his eyes. "Fine, ya write wherever ya write, and I'll hang out in yer den and avail myself of yer library. How's that?"

The picture was more appealing than she wanted to admit. Very appealing. Gavin and his sock feet in her recliner, soaking in the fire from the hearth while he read a paperback? How sexy was that? Too sexy, in her opinion. She might get attached to a sexy like that.

Then again, he'd be close. He'd be flirting. Who knew what could happen in a week? She wasn't looking for anything long-term, especially with someone from halfway across the world, but hadn't she just been bemoaning the lack of romance and orgasms in her life? He hadn't offered orgasms, but he might.

Scarlett took a sip of her margarita, thinking hard. By the time she swallowed, her decision had been made.

"Sounds like a plan to me. What do you want to do first?"

CHAPTER
Five

"What are we doin' again?"

Scarlett shot him a mischievous glance. "Just hold your arms up."

Gavin grumbled under his breath but put his arms in the air, allowing Scarlett to tie the apron around his waist. "We don' really need these, do we?"

Claire giggled where she stood behind the decorating table, looking on. "Of course you do."

When she held up her phone and clicked a quick picture, he growled in her direction. "Why aren't you wearin' an apron?"

"Because I'm the expert." She waggled her brows at him.

"Expert at fibbin'," he griped good-naturedly. Truth be told, he didn't mind the apron at all. In fact he wore one frequently when he cooked at home just to keep his clothes clean. A habit his gran had been the one to ingrain in him.

"Okay," Scarlett said, her amusement as obvious as Claire's. "Time for decorating."

Gavin bent down, bringing his mouth close to her ear—and allowing her sweet sugar scent to fill his nose. "I take it you've done this before?"

Scarlett turned toward him, bringing them face-to-face. Or nose-to-nose. "Why is it that everything you say sounds dirty?"

It's a gift. "Because everyone around me has a dirty mind?" He couldn't resist; he nipped the delicate tip of her nose.

"Hey!"

He straightened. "Hay is for horses, my gran always said."

Scarlett rubbed at her nose, but he noticed she looked about as upset with him as he'd been with the apron. "Did she spank your bottom for being naughty, too?"

"Course not. I was a perfect angel." He let his grin break through. "Sounds kinky though."

Scarlett backhanded him in the stomach, drawing an *oof* with the impact. "Ice your gingerbread man and stop being…"

He raised a brow when she paused. "Stop being…what?"

"Stop being…you!"

He chuckled as he drew a plate holding a naked gingerbread man cookie close to him. "That might be hard ta accomplish, but I'll try." He looked over the array of bags and plates of sprinkles and candies scattered over the table they were standing at. "Where do we start?"

Since Claire had moved to the next table down to help a couple of young lads with their gingerbread men, he let Scarlett instruct him. Of course, watching her handle the plump bags of icing was… Well, he best get his mind on other things, hadn't he?

"This is royal icing," she was saying as she traced the outer edge of her cookie with a line from the bag.

"Apropos."

She gave him a side-eye. "You outline the area you want iced, then use the flood icing to flood the space. It dries smooth." After completing the line, she switched to a different bag and began to fill the space inside it with a thinner icing. The puddle of white pooled out to meet the edge, contained by the original line she'd drawn.

"Flood. Got it." He eyed his gingerbread man, whose one leg appeared to be slightly offset. "I think my man here has an issue."

Scarlett was focused on the icing she was slowly spreading over her gingerbread woman's skirt. The tip of her pink tongue stuck out between her plump lips, giving him ideas he shouldn't be having with ten-year-olds in close proximity. "Uh-huh," was all she said.

He should've taken the time to give himself a good wank before leaving the mansion this morning. His rest had been deep, but the morning hours had been filled with a dream about Scarlett that had stuck his mind in directions he was having trouble pulling away from now, with her so close to him. Like how to best put that tongue to use. How to show her exactly where he'd like her to be focused—on him, not a silly cookie.

He rolled his eyes. Striving to focus on something besides the tightness behind his zipper, he pursed his lips and began to whistle, releasing a merry holiday tune as he adjusted the limbs on his gingerbread man. He began with the black icing. Then some red. He popped a bit of one leg into his mouth and enjoyed the sharp flavor of the ginger and clove as he continued decorating. Claire was bonnie one in the kitchen; his tastebuds attested to that.

A pair of candy buttons came next, for eyes. A small licorice mouth, opened wide to scream—the rest of the licorice went down his throat along with the cookie bits. By the time he added some coconut hair, tinted with green food coloring (that was probably provided for grass, not a rockin' hairstyle), Scarlett was almost finished with her gingerbread woman.

ELLA SHERIDAN

"What do ya think?" he asked, anticipation filling him at her reaction.

Pulling her gaze from her plate, Scarlett shifted over to his. Her eyes rounded with far more drama than he deemed necessary. "Gavin!"

"Aye?"

She sputtered. "I'm— You—"

"That good, eh?"

Claire walked over to see what they were doing, and burst into laughter. "I should've known it would be you."

He pretended to be affronted, hiding his lurking grin. "What would be me?"

She gestured to his plate. "You would be the one to make your gingerbread man do something besides just stand there."

"Standin' there is borin'." He looked down at his cookie. His gingerbread man was dressed in a black karate gi, a yellow belt around his middle. Green coconut hair stuck out in every direction, and one leg was raised as if to kick an opponent.

Not very effectively given that the leg was a bloody stump. So was one hand. And his head might be coming off too.

He swiped at the blood dripping down one side of the cookie's neck and brought it up to his mouth. "I think it's perfect." The icing tasted sweet on his tongue, sweeter than the cookie.

"You would," Scarlett said, amusement filling her voice. "Such a little-boy thing to do."

He leaned into her space. "But it made you laugh."

Her cheeks turned pink at his proximity. "Yes, you did. You seem to do that a lot."

"Good." Laughter was the best aphrodisiac in the world in his opinion.

He dared to brush a kiss along that tempting cheek.

36

The door to the shop opened behind them, the little bell above it sending a sweet chime through the air. Gavin looked over his shoulder to see Scarlett's friend Iris walking through. She was a lovely middle-aged woman with thick, light gray hair cut in a stylish sweep over her forehead, short on the sides and back to reveal an elegant neck. The glasses she wore were perfect for a librarian, a modern version of the old horn-rimmed style in a sexy red that did wonderful things for her fair complexion. Unfortunately right now, the eyes behind those glasses seemed worried.

"Iris!" Claire called happily before frowning. "Is everything all right? Aren't you about to do the gift exchange at the library?"

"We are, but…" She hurried in their direction. "I was hoping Lincoln was here?"

"Unfortunately not," Claire said. "He ran to Gatlinburg to pick up some supplies I needed for the wedding cake."

Iris looked as if she was about to cry.

"What's the matter?" Scarlett asked.

Iris was literally wringing her hands. He thought people only did that in books. "Ernesto was supposed to play Santa today for us to hand out the gifts to the children, but he called to say he was in a fender bender and can't make it." She gestured down her body. "I'm definitely not going to fit the Santa costume, even with my heels."

"Not unless you roll up the arms and legs way more than is practical," Claire agreed.

"I was hoping Lincoln would play Santa. The kids have so been looking forward to this, and I want to make everything special for them, but…"

Gavin cleared his throat. "If you need a gentleman…might I volunteer?"

Iris eyed him warily. "The library is hosting kids from a foundation that supports children in foster care. A lot of kids.

They can get a bit…rowdy when so many of them are in one place. How are you with noisy kids?"

"None of my own," he informed her. "But my stepsiblings have ten or eleven wee ones—I've lost count at this point—between the lot of them. I can handle a few mischief-makin' bairns."

Iris gave him what was probably her best librarian's look. Twenty years ago that look would have cowed him. "More than a few."

Gavin waved her concerns away. "I'll do it. Lead me to the costume."

Which was how he found himself with a fat pillow strapped to his lean belly and a thick red coat covering him. Scarlett adjusted the silky white beard fastened over his ears. "You do Santa well," she told him with a wink. "Must be the mischief-maker in you. I don't think you're too far off from those kids out there, Mr. Karate Disaster Cookie."

"You thought my cookie was hilarious." He stroked the white hair hanging down over his chin. "I've always wondered about growin' a beard."

She plopped the red hat onto his head, then stepped back, taking in the picture he made from head to toe. "Somehow I don't see it as a permanent fixture in your future."

"I'll stick to stubble then. Never had any complaints about that."

Scarlett flushed that pretty pink. "Behave."

"Me? Never!" He chuckled, then cast around for the cart Iris had pointed out. "Let's get these presents delivered. The children are waitin'!"

The community room of the library was filled to over-flowing with kids of all ages and the volunteers who hope-lessly tried to wrangle them. When Santa appeared, screams of joy filled the room. A few of the babes began to cry at the sight of him, uncertain why a big man with a long beard calling out loud, "Ho ho ho's," was drawing near. Gavin stepped carefully around the fearful ones and made his way to the front of the room and the Christmas tree waiting there for him, sparkling with cheery colored lights and homemade ornaments.

"Hey, aren't you supposed to have the presents in a bag?" one tough guy of about eight said as Gavin pulled the wagon full of toys to the front.

"Yeah, where's Santa's bag?" another frowning boy asked. The two were joined by a small pack of troublemakers jostling each other and stepping on too many of the younger ones as they jockeyed for attention.

Gavin waited for a lull in the action to speak.

Crouching near the boys' level, he gestured them forward with a crooked finger. The boys' approached hesitantly.

"Ya want ta see Santa's bag, I take it?"

Confusion seemed to fill the small group as they took in his accent. Here was something foreign to them, unfamiliar, something they couldn't proclaim proudly to know all about. It gave him an edge he hurried to take advantage of.

"Santa's helpers couldn't come today, and they forgot ta send the presents in my bag. All I have is this wagon, ya see." He gestured to the pile of presents. "But I also don' have helpers. Would you boys like to be my helpers today?"

Intrigued with the idea of being given special status, the boys channeled their energy into handing out presents before taking their own into a corner of the room to tear open. There was no order here, only chaos and a sea of paper and gift bags and toy wrappings as children dug for their prize and happily ignored the mess. Gavin had never seen anything so satisfying. So many little faces full of stress and wariness when he'd entered, now smiling and carefree as they played with their presents. Many of them wanted Gavin to help open their toys, tear off the wrappers, and while he was occupied with them, Scarlett disappeared from his side. He saw her later helping the volunteers tidy the mess. She came back once the chaos was somewhat tamed, only to find him cuddling a sleepy little girl with thick black ringlets in her hair and her thumb in her mouth.

He shrugged at Scarlett's tender look. The wee one had sought him out, exhausted, and curled into his arms as if she knew him. Maybe she did in a way, from the tales of Christmas she'd likely heard all her life.

"You did a good job, Santa," she told him, rubbing the little girl's back.

"I think I put my audience to sleep," he joked.

"It's the excitement. Wears 'em out every time."

He scanned her face, trying to read beyond the surface. "Do ya have children?"

"No, that wasn't for me. I need too much thinking time." She gave him a smile that said she was content with her choice. "But I've had plenty of friends with little ones, so I know the drill. Here." She eased the little girl out of his arms. "I'll return her to her keeper while you go change."

He made quick work of switching back into his own clothes, and when he returned to the community room, he found the children happily lined up, ready to load into the buses with their toys in hand. Iris thanked him profusely, which he shook his head at. "Happy I could help."

"Well you certainly did," she told him, giving him a sweetly scented hug that reminded him of Scarlett, if somewhat muted. "Thank you."

"Anytime." He took Scarlett's hand, and they headed out to retrieve their cookies from the bakery. "Ready to write?" he asked her. "I need my story, after all."

She laughed. "You won't get it for a little while." But her steps were bouncy and her smile happy as they walked back to her place for the afternoon.

CHAPTER
Six

The walk from the bakery to Scarlett's house was cold, but they warmed up when they got back with sub sandwiches and warm cider and their gingerbread cookies. She was used to spending a lot of time alone, but being with Gavin didn't seem to drain her like a lot of socializing did. And oddly enough, it felt completely natural to leave him in her living room after lunch, piled into the recliner near the fireplace to read—yes, in his sock feet, though she had no whisky for him to sip—while she went into the office to write. She didn't often have people in her space when she was being creative, but Gavin didn't feel like an invasive presence. He felt natural. She knew his smile would charm her when she came back out, and he would make her laugh. In fact, she went into her next chapter anticipating seeing him again.

Her office held a chaise where she curled up with a warm blanket, her laptop, and headphones over her ears. Every book had a playlist she played on repeat, although sometimes her creativity would get stuck on a song and she would play just that one for hours while she wrote. Sometimes she became stuck and would dance around with her headphones

ELLA SHERIDAN

on until inspiration struck again, although she didn't dare risk that with Gavin in the house. She'd had some embarrassing moments when she first moved into the house and forgot to close the curtains in her office before her dancing sessions. Her neighbors were used to her by now, but that didn't make it any less embarrassing—though not nearly as much as showing Gavin her birthday suit the first second they'd met. She didn't think she'd ever get over that.

With her headphones on, she wasn't certain how long Gavin knocked on her door later that day. At some point she became vaguely aware of a loud sound and looked up, surfacing slowly from her deep dive into her story to the real world. When she tugged her headphones off, she realized he was knocking on the office door. "Come in."

Gavin tucked his head inside to peek at her. "I wasn't certain if interruptin' was all right, but ya've been at it for almost five hours."

She stood, feeling every minute of those five hours in her tight muscles as she stretched. "Sorry."

He opened the door farther and leaned against the doorframe, arms crossed over his chest in a way that made his muscles pop and her drool. "No need to be sorry. It's just that Linc called and asked if they could bring pizza for dinner."

A smile of relief broke across her face. "I was figuring I'd have to cook."

He frowned. "I'm perfectly capable of feeding us, lass."

The thought gave her pause. Or rather, the image—Gavin in her kitchen, stirring something on the stove, those sexy curls falling over his forehead. Nix the shirt and the picture became a fantasy that made her insides warm and her cheeks get hot.

"What was that thought?"

She jerked her gaze back to Gavin and reality. "Nothing."

His eyes narrowed. "I'm thinkin' it was more than nothin', but we can talk about that later. Right now...pizza?"

She pushed his demand to discuss her fantasies away and focused on now. "Lincoln and Claire's pizzas are ambrosia, so definitely yes."

He chuckled. "How about ya wrap up and I'll get things ready in the meantime."

Resisting the urge to follow him into the kitchen, she nodded. "Sure."

She settled back into her spot, now aware of how stiff she was, and finished off the paragraph she'd been working on. A few notes on the direction she intended to go so she wouldn't be lost when she sat down for tomorrow's writing session, and she was ready to stop. By the time she exited the office, she could hear voices down the hall.

Claire greeted her when she entered the kitchen. "How's the book coming?"

"Good," Scarlett answered. "About four chapters and I'll be done."

"And then she's goin' to tell me what's happened to Levi and Abby," Gavin put in.

"You've read her books?" Linc asked, seeming surprised.

"O' course. Just one so far, the first in this..." He waved a hand as if looking for the right word.

"Duet," Scarlett supplied. "When you have a pair of books that go together in romance, it's typically called a duet."

"Right, duet. And it was excellent"—Gavin frowned her way—"even if it did end on a cliffhanger."

Claire grimaced. "I hate it when she does that."

"You know you love it," Scarlett put in. "It keeps you clamoring for the next book."

"It's the months in between that drive me nuts," Claire explained.

"Right?" Gavin asked. "How could she do that to us?"

"Very easily," Scarlett said, grinning as she moved past the trio toward the counter bar. Two pizzas steamed inside insulated bags, and when Scarlett lifted a lid, her mouth watered.

Better than the best Italian she'd had anywhere else. She understood why Linc was famous for his food, although Claire gave him a run for his money.

Linc handed her a plate. "Sounds like a bit of a masochist," he said, eyeing her. She could feel the wariness in him now, as if he didn't quite know what to make of this mild-mannered woman he suddenly realized had a penchant for causing others psychological pain.

She grinned, enjoying his shock. How was it none of her friends' significant others had realized this before now? "You have no idea how right you are."

They piled pizza onto their plates and took them to the living room since Scarlett's breakfast nook was too small for all four of them. Linc added small salads, and Claire followed with four bottles of Stone IPA, a SoCal beer Lincoln had discovered on his many trips to California that had quickly become a favorite.

"When do you start filming, Linc?" Gavin asked. Lincoln was a guest judge on a popular TV cooking competition—mostly made popular by women who watched just for a glimpse of Lincoln—and filming for the next season should begin soon in Cali.

"February."

From what Scarlett understood, he'd be in California for six to eight weeks for the full season to be completed. A glance at Claire showed her friend frowning down at her pizza. "It must be hard, being apart so much."

Lincoln's gaze snapped to Claire as well. He swallowed his bite of pizza and reached for his girlfriend's hand. "It is." The two exchanged a look. "But my contract with the film company is up after this year, and we can renegotiate."

"Do you know what you'll do yet?" Gavin asked.

Lincoln shrugged. "Depends on what they offer me. It would have to be much better than my girl here, and I don't see that happening."

Scarlett knew Claire already missed Linc. His world-class restaurant in New York City required his presence on a regular basis, as well as the many appearances he made for the charity he represented. He was gone often, and getting away from Black Wolf's Bluff was difficult for Claire, especially now that she had two Gimme Sugar locations to manage. The resort JD and his friends were building hadn't opened yet, but they were on track for it in a few short months. By spring of next year Claire would have the second store up and running, and though Scarlett had met her new store manager, she knew from her own experience that handing over her creation to someone else to take care of was never easy. She loved her publishing team, but that didn't mean trusting their handling of her "babies" was ever without its own complications. It required constant oversight and input on top of the creation process itself.

"I'm surprised we haven't heard from Carter today," Scarlett mused. Gavin had spent all day with her instead of his best friend.

Lincoln frowned. "JD said Erin went home early today."

"Everything okay at home?" Scarlett asked Claire. They'd all been concerned when Erin's father had a heart scare just a couple of months ago.

Claire shook her head. "Erin wasn't feeling well."

"Will she be all right for the weddin'?" Gavin asked.

Something sparked in Claire's eyes that Scarlett couldn't interpret. "I don't think it's serious."

They demolished most of the two pizzas before piling up on the couches to enjoy the fire. Scarlett returned from a bathroom break to find the men discussing Gavin's work.

"Business is booming," Gavin was saying, "even with Carter dividing his time."

"What exactly is your work?" Claire asked.

"International finance, which is a fancy way of saying we handle investments all over the world. The details can be boring, but I work on the international part of the business, clients who are not located on US soil, so it involves a lot of travel. I can be in Japan one week and Norway the next."

Scarlett couldn't imagine.

"Sounds like a lot of jet lag," Claire said.

Gavin chuckled. "There is that."

"How long will you do that?" Linc asked. "You have, what, fifteen years till retirement?"

"Give or take, though Carter and I have discussed early retirement."

Linc's brows hit his hairline. "For both of you?"

Gavin nodded. "There are a lot of hungry up-and-comers in our business, with a lot more energy than me, and we've managed to acquire a few with a lot of talent. I've got a group I've been mentorin', but nothin' has been decided yet. I'd love to keep travelin', but I'd also like to spend more than a few days at any location. And at home."

"With family?" Claire asked. Scarlett eyed her friend, wondering if her questions were idle curiosity or if she was drawing information out for Scarlett's benefit. Claire had spoken with Gavin before, after all. The four men frequently video chatted, and Scarlett knew the women were included whenever they were around.

"No," Gavin said. "I'm not close to family. Carter's the closest thing to family I have."

He said he wasn't close, not that he didn't have any. He'd told Iris he had stepsiblings and their children. Something about his family didn't lend itself to closeness then. She wondered why.

It sounded lonely, all that travel and his friends scattered across the world, but she had a feeling Gavin wasn't. And she got it. She had no family left either—she was an only child, and her parents had died in an accident while she was in college. No grandparents still alive. It was how she'd ended up in Black Wolf's Bluff, a choice that had allowed her to meet her own found family—Erin, Claire, Lily, Iris.

"Ever thought of moving to the States, or any of the places you've traveled to?"

Her ears couldn't help perking up at Claire's question, but Gavin was shaking his head. "Can't." A small smile appeared on his lips. "There is something different about Scotland, even the crowded urban parts. There's nothing like it. The air itself feels different. And when I can get out of the city…well, it's home, ya know? No matter where I go, I'll always come back to her."

Scarlett loved her little home, this town, but what Gavin had…it was special. "That's beautiful, Gavin."

He winked. "Remember that for your next alpha hero."

"Alpha hero?" Linc asked.

"Have you been reading up on the romance genre, Gavin?" Claire asked.

"I have had a sudden surge of interest," he admitted, grinning. But the way he looked at Scarlett made her wonder if he wasn't talking about more than a book.

CHAPTER
Seven

J D told Gavin at breakfast that the temperature was expected to drop the next day, just in time for Christmas. Despite the walks he and Scarlett had taken around town, Gavin was itching to get outside. A quick text with Scarlett and she agreed to show him some trails in the nearby Smoky Mountain National Park.

Gavin had visited Nashville several times, but the beauty of the city could not compare to the wilderness he and Scarlett found themselves surrounded by that morning. The air was crisp but not frigid, the trees breaking up any wind that would freeze them out and filtering the sunlight to a soft glow around them. Scarlett led the way on the trail, the surety of her movements telling him she spent a good bit of time out here. As they moved, she warmed and unbuttoned her coat, then tied it around her waist, giving him a better view of her curvy body.

Talk about beauty.

"Tell me about your life, lass. What do you do besides write?" he asked as they traversed a stack of moss-covered boulders crowding against the trail.

Scarlett paused, a hand on a boulder to steady herself as she looked over her shoulder. "My life?"

"O' course." He found himself holding his breath as he waited to hear more about the intriguing woman who had somehow managed to cross his path in this tiny little town.

She continued along the trail. "This is pretty much it, Gavin." She stepped over a tangle of roots and began a downward descent. "I'm nowhere near as exciting as you."

"I don' believe that at all."

She pushed her sleeves up. "I write books, go to the pub and dance with my friends on Thursday nights, help out Iris in the library sometimes. Hike. Visit the café every now and again. Life is pretty simple."

"Did you always want to live in a small town?"

"Yes." Grabbing ahold of a tree trunk as she turned a corner, she shot him a smile. "I'm not one of those people who wants to stay cooped up all the time. It does nothing for my creativity. And though I enjoy people, I'm happy without the crowds. Maybe that's the thing about traveling. I used to think a lot about exciting adventures and exotic locales, even wrote some stories based in faraway places, but let's face it, it's not as much fun to travel alone, especially for those of us who aren't extreme extroverts." She gave him a look.

Now that he couldn't deny. "Caught that, did ya?"

"Everyone catches that about you, Gavin. It's hard to miss."

"And part of what makes me so lovable?"

He shouldn't have used that word—the cardinal sin of any short-term relationship, to use the L-word in any form—but it had slipped out with no warning. Scarlett seemed to do that to him, make him forget things like rules and watching his tongue.

"Like a big teddy bear, ya are," she joked, adopting a heavy caricature of his light brogue. He couldn't help laughing.

"Anyway, it's also not as safe for women to travel alone. I'd do it in a group, and the girls and I have taken some short trips, but nowhere too far." She shrugged. "I can't expect someone who's been to so many exotic locations to understand."

He understood better than she might think. "Where's the most exotic place ya've been?"

"Florida." A chuckle escaped her. "I've never been overseas, though I've traveled a bit in the US. Lily and Claire and I went on a girls' trip for a week to the Florida Keys a couple of years ago. And Savannah. In Georgia, you know?" She made a low humming sound at his nod. "I love the atmosphere there, though I'm less about beaches than I am about woods and mountains. But I'll visit anywhere once."

She would love the Highlands, he knew it. And the Scottish beaches —they weren't like Florida, though that made them more of a draw in his opinion.

Why was he considering where Scarlett would enjoy traveling? Sure, he could share suggestions, but when he imagined her in Scotland, it wasn't with anyone at her side but him—and that would definitely take them past the one-week deadline he gave himself with any woman. So why was he considering it? And yet he couldn't deny that he was, indeed, considering it.

They hadn't even slept together. He hoped sex was on the table—he was strongly attracted to her, and old enough and experienced enough that he saw no point in delayed gratification. Yet even not having that experience with her, he was daydreaming about more time.

Scarlett was oblivious to his musings, thank goodness. "It's not like I've settled," she was saying. "I don't want you to think that. I enjoy my life." Another pause as she scrambled over a fallen log. "Somewhere along the way I think I settled into work and my fictional worlds and forgot things like exploring castles in Scotland."

"Ya want to visit some castles, lass?"

She shrugged. "I did. Do. An adventure now and then wouldn't be a PITA."

"A PITA?"

"Pain in the ass."

Gavin snickered. "Travel can indeed be a PITA." He hesitated. The words on the tip of his tongue went against every rule he'd made for himself, and yet they beat at him to be spoken. Finally he gave his caution a silent *fuck it* and spoke. "I wouldn't mind smoothin' the way if ya wanted to see some castles."

Scarlett stumbled. When he gripped her arm, steadying her, she turned wide eyes up to him. "Gavin, are you offering to travel with me?"

She had to point it out, didn't she. Yet, rather than ramping up, the nerves in his gut settled with her question.

"I think it would be a pleasure, not a pain."

They stood like that, frozen in the moment, until a snapping branch caught their attention. Just down the hill, a small deer stepped from around a tree. Her—at least he assumed it was her, given there were no horns—hide was the same soft brown as the bark, neatly camouflaging her from predators. If it hadn't been for the fallen limb she'd stumbled over, they would likely never have seen her.

"Oh," Scarlett breathed, nearly silent.

He took her hand in his, squeezing to communicate his delight as the deer crossed to a tiny patch of green left over from summer and had a nibble. Several minutes passed before a distant noise startled the creature, sending her bounding into the woods. Gavin gestured in the direction she'd gone. "I can see the draw of this place."

Scarlett started up their walk again. Up ahead waited a tiny wooden bridge that arched over a lightly trickling stream. She stopped in the middle to look over one side. "This is one of the reasons I bought my house. Did you know that water helps with creative flow? Most creatives find they get ideas in the shower or bath, sitting near a stream, listening to the rain." She tipped her head as if listening to the movement below them. "Having the Salalai River flow right next to my house means I can go outside and hear the water anytime I want." She grinned. "Plus I only have neighbors on one side."

He lived in an apartment in Edinburgh, so that was a luxury he wasn't afforded. "Always a bonus."

"Yes." She leaned against the bridge railing. "Unfortunately they're on the same side as my office window."

"Why is that unfortunate?"

He propped an elbow on the railing, facing her, and noticed a pink blush coloring her cheeks. Her hesitation had him leaning close, bringing his mouth to her ear. "Tell me your secrets, Scarlett."

"My secrets are embarrassing."

He chuckled. "Like flashing a Scotsman in your kitchen? That was sexy, not embarrassing. I definitely wouldn't object to you doing it again."

Her eyes shot up to meet his. "Gavin!"

He shrugged, refusing to apologize. "Only the truth. Now, what secrets do you have about your neighbors?"

She turned her gaze back out to the stream. "So…I have this habit."

He propped his head in his hand. "Do tell."

"When I get stuck on a story, I…" Her blush deepened. "Well, I dance."

"You dance?"

"Yeah." She glanced at him from the corner of her eye before looking away again. "I dance around my office with my headphones on until a new idea comes into my head."

He guessed he could see how that might be embarrassing to her.

"The music blocks everything out, and…"

"And?"

She dropped her face into her hands and mumbled something he couldn't make out.

"What was that, lass?"

She let her hands fall away but kept her head down. "I sometimes forget I'm in my pajamas while I write. Or my robe. Or a towel. And I don't always remember to close the curtains."

He imagined the scenario in his head and nearly groaned at the need that stirred in his gut. Seriously, could this woman get any cuter? "I bet they got an eyeful, though I can attest that it's a pleasant eyeful."

"Gavin!" She backhanded his stomach lightly.

He caught her hand, holding it against him. "What? Would you rather I said the view was hideous?" He stepped closer, bringing Scarlett's shoulder against his chest. "That would be an outright lie, so yeah, not goin' to do that."

A sudden look of horror crossed her face. "You haven't told JD and Lincoln and Carter about that, have you?"

Her fear drew out the need to protect her—not just from a rumor, but from anything that might come her way. He drew her full into his arms, turning her to face him. "Now why would I share a memory like that with them?" He tugged her chin up until her eyes met his. "I'm not in the habit o' tellin' my male friends what turns me on."

She opened her mouth, but no words came out.

"What?" He chuckled. "You can't believe you don' attract me, Scarlett. I've been open about that, surely?"

She still didn't respond.

"Guess I'll prove it then." Without hesitation he ducked his head and took her mouth.

She tasted as good as she smelled. A hint of coffee and cream beneath the fresh taste of toothpaste. Her vanilla scent filled his nose even as her body molded to his, relaxing as he drew her tight against him. Soft breasts, soft stomach, hips he could get a good grip on—she was everything he enjoyed in a woman. He parted her lips with his and licked inside, tasting her more deeply. A groan rumbled through him.

Not wanting to take things too far, too fast, he eased back. Scarlett stood in the circle of his arms, eyes closed, still as a statue. After a moment he began to get concerned. "Scarlett?"

She remained as she was but finally spoke. "God, Gavin."

"What does that mean?"

She blinked her eyes open. "You are lethal."

Relief cracked open in his chest, and he grinned. "As good as yer heroes?"

"Better. You're real."

"Now that is a compliment indeed." One he wouldn't forget anytime soon. It wasn't often you were told you were better than a woman's fantasies.

"Kiss me again."

The demand firmed his cock even more than the kiss had. And their second kiss… Well, he was forced to keep that one short. Anything more and he'd be looking for someplace for them to sneak off the trail to.

When they resumed their hike, it was with Scarlett's hand in his, fingers linked tight.

CHAPTER
Eight

Writing went well that afternoon once Scarlett was able to immerse herself, but it took a little while. The memory of Gavin's kiss, his taste, his body made it difficult to concentrate. And that comment about seeing the castles…

She'd assumed that he was doing nothing more than passing the time while he was in town. Had she considered sex with him? Of course she had—she'd have to be dead not to. But she hadn't considered anything beyond this week.

Gavin lived overseas. She had a life here. For anything casual, the difficulties didn't seem worth it. She might, somewhere deep down, question what it would be like to be his; she was a romantic, after all. But it wasn't realistic. She needed to keep viewing this situation without any rose-colored glasses. No matter what happened this week, that's all this was—short-term fun.

Finally, two chapters later, she stood and stretched the aches from her body, then exited the office. In the living room she found Gavin asleep in the recliner, one of her books open on his lap. He looked like a little boy playing grown-up, curls falling over his forehead, those compelling eyes hidden by sleep. His long body was relaxed beneath the blanket, his sock-covered feet sticking off the edge of her chair. No drooling or snoring for this guy, definitely. The urge to smooth his hair back, discover for herself if it was as soft as it looked, if his stubble felt as good against her skin as she imagined it would, rose inside her. Gavin was worming his way beneath her guard. She'd started the week teasing the ultimate playboy, but seeing him like this evoked both tenderness and desire. The latter she could deal with, but the former…?

She was working on a simple soup-and-salad dinner when a sleepy Gavin padded into the kitchen half an hour later. "You're awake."

"Sorry," he said roughly, running his fingers through the mussed curls on his head. "Jet lag and fresh air puts me right out every time."

"I imagine so." She gestured to dinner. "Pretty basic, but are you hungry?"

His eyes sharpened on her the slightest bit, turning him from little-boy cute to grown-man sexy in an instant. "Definitely."

For some reason that one word made her belly clench. She cleared her throat. "Okay."

Her croaked response brought a smile to his full lips. Trying not to think too much about his lips—or stare at them —she gestured him back to the living room. "Want to look for a Christmas movie while I set the table? We can watch after we eat."

Gavin complied but gave her a knowing grin on his way out.

After dinner Scarlett plated up a couple of brownies she'd gotten from Claire's bakery, heated them, then added a scoop of eggnog-flavored ice cream on the side. She topped the desserts with a couple of Hershey kisses as Gavin finished placing their dinner dishes in the dishwasher. Without thinking, she commented, "There's nothing sexier than a man washing dishes."

Gavin straightened. His eyes had turned whisky bright, trained on her with an intensity that dried out her mouth. "Nothing at all?"

Well, when you look at me that way… "Nothing," she said hoarsely.

One side of his mouth quirked up. "That little white lie might get you in trouble."

When he started across the kitchen toward her, she snatched up the dessert bowls with a squeak. "Ready for the movie?"

Gavin trailed her into the living room, chuckling at her lack of courage.

"What did you pick?" she asked, moving to the couch. The sight of Macaulay Culkin frozen on the screen made her smile.

"*Home Alone.* It's my favorite Christmas movie."

"Somehow that doesn't surprise me." She passed Gavin his bowl as he sat next to her. "Why is it your favorite?"

"Just look at him." Gavin pointed to the image of "Kevin," his hair spiked from a bath, mouth open wide as he gave his trademark "Aaaah!" "He's so damn cute; Who wouldn't love him?"

He had a point. And though she struggled with the way Kevin's family treated him at the beginning of the movie, it always warmed her heart to see their view of him and their relationships shift over the course of the two hours. Not to mention, Kevin's antics with the robbers and Joe Pesci's fake cursing were hilarious.

They sat back on the couch, thighs and shoulders touching, and dug into their desserts as the movie began. When their bowls were empty, Gavin placed them on the coffee table, gathered her against his side, and laid back into the corner of the couch, stretching out his long legs beside the bowls and pulling Scarlett's body to recline alongside his. Cuddling.

Oh God, they were cuddling, and it felt. So. Good. She loved cuddling—in fact, aside from sex, it might be the thing she enjoyed most about dating—but most men weren't natural cuddlers. She should have known Gavin would be. The man seemed instinctively good at anything a woman might desire, so it made sense that he was a perfect cuddler.

A long sigh escaped as she relaxed, molding her body to his side.

The onscreen antics had Gavin chuckling throughout the movie, the laughter rumbling from his chest to vibrate through her body. The longer it lasted, the more she felt her hunger ramping up, and not for food. Gavin's muscles were heavy, his torso firm against her softness, reminding her of the feel of a man's weight on top of her. Of how soft his mouth had been this afternoon, the perfect contrast to his body. Two kisses hadn't been enough this afternoon; they'd been an appetizer that only made her eager for more. She hadn't intended this as a Netflix-and-chill opportunity, but if Gavin felt the same hunger she did?

She didn't think she'd turn him down.

As Kevin prepped his house for the finale, she tried to resist the urge to squirm against Gavin. Was it getting hot in here? Please, don't let that be a hot flash creeping up. Which reminded her, had she shaved her legs—and other important things— in the shower this morning? Was she really having this internal monologue while Gavin seemed completely absorbed in the movie? She needed to get ahold of herself before she got her hopes up about things she really didn't need to be thinking about right at this moment.

Onscreen, Kevin grasped his brother's tarantula and placed it on the robber's face. Gavin laughed so hard at the man's scream that she thought he might fall off the couch. His amusement had her chuckling right alongside him.

"You were probably exactly like Kevin as a kid, weren't you?"

Grappling his laughter under control, Gavin shook his head. "No, my da wouldn't have put up with any nonsense. But what little boy didn't dream of playing pirates? Protecting his booty, setting booby traps for the enemy?" He turned his back on the screen, snuggled down on the couch, and laid his head on her chest, wide, innocent eyes staring up at her. "Then we got older and fell into other booby traps."

A bark of laughter left her. "That is a terrible pun. Just terrible."

He rubbed his chin lightly over her breast, the hard line of his jaw catching her suddenly hard nipple through her shirt. "It made ya laugh, didn' it? It couldn't have been that bad then."

Her breath cut off in her throat. That touch... Laughter forgotten, she stared into those wicked amber eyes and forgot all the questions and concerns and silly little scenarios rolling through her head. All that mattered was that look and those lips and getting more of that touch.

"Gavin..."

Reaching up, he tangled his fingers into her hair and urged her head down to meet his. "Scarlett."

Their breath mingled as lips brushed lightly against each other. Gavin's tongue flicked against her bottom lip. "Come down here."

She scooched down until their bodies aligned perfectly. Gavin curled one leg over hers and pulled until their limbs were scissored together. Against the front of her thigh, a hard length made itself known.

So he hadn't been as involved in the movie as she'd thought. When she pressed her thigh against him, Gavin's eyes closed, a flush of desire rising along his cheekbones. "Ye're dangerous, lass."

Her lips tugged up into a smile. "I don't think it's me

who's dangerous. When I said you were lethal this afternoon, I meant it." He was. Pressed between him and the back of the couch, overwhelmed by his body, his scent, his sheer presence, she knew for a fact that she'd been right—and now all she wanted to do was revel in it. In him.

Gavin pushed one arm beneath her neck, hooking it around to hold her upper body firmly against him. The other hand went to her hip, gripping, then down to her ass. "Ye're a luscious handful, Scarlett." He squeezed. "Ya feel good against me."

She did a little exploring of her own, found the hem of his Henley, and slid her hand beneath it. His back was smooth, warm. Hard. Digging her fingers in barely made an impression. She arched closer. "You do too."

He didn't waste any more time on compliments, for which she was grateful. His mouth descended on hers, and then she was experiencing his kiss again—that mobile mouth, the taste of chocolate and something distinctly him, that agile tongue. She loved kissing, and Gavin was the best kiss she'd ever received. Time passed, seconds falling into each other without awareness as she lost herself in that kiss. Only his touch on her bare skin brought her back to reality.

One firm hand slid beneath her shirt, long fingers gliding along her side. Up, then down. Up, then down. So close to where she truly wanted him, but so far away at the same time.

"Is this all right?" he asked.

She bit her lip. Nodded. Her body rolled into him, undulating in a way she couldn't control. "More, Gavin."

He grinned. Coming up on his elbow, he ducked his head into the hollow of her neck and shoulder and began to nibble along the sensitive skin there. Scarlett threw her head back, giving him room, delighting in the zing of pleasure flowing from her throat to her nipples to her core. And when his hand swept up to her breast? She groaned. "Yes."

Gavin nudged aside the fabric, his fingers finding her bare tip. A cry left her as he pinched the rigid nub. Her fingernails dug into his back.

The doorbell rang.

Both of them froze. Surely she hadn't heard that. No way would someone be dropping by her house *right now,* right when she and Gavin were about to—

Ding-dong.

"Shit." Gavin shuddered against her.

Her thought exactly.

"Can we get away with ignorin' them?"

She clenched her eyes shut. "TV's on. Lights are on. I'd say no."

A knock sounded on the door. "Gavin! Scarlett!"

Carter. Gavin cursed again. Sitting up, he withdrew his hand from her bra with a look of deep regret. "I need a minute."

She bet he did. "I'll get the door."

Gavin stood, his pants tented in the front, then bent back down to give her one desperate, hungry kiss before he gathered their dishes and hurried down the hall toward the kitchen. Scarlett stood. "Coming!" she yelled through gritted teeth.

After straightening her clothes, she took a few deep breaths, willed her libido to calm the f— down, and walked to the door.

On the porch, Carter, Erin, and Thad stood grinning. Erin's face held a peaceful glow. "I was finally feeling better, so we thought we'd stop by and spend some time with you guys." She glanced around Scarlett's shoulder. "Is that okay?"

What am I going to say, "No, we were about to have sex"? She glanced down at Thad's eager face. Definitely not saying that. And Erin looked so happy to be out and about. How could she say no? "Of course it's okay." She stepped back and swung the door open. "Come on in."

As the trio piled into the living room, Gavin returned from the kitchen. A quick glance told her he'd gotten his excitement under control, though he did still look the slightest bit flushed. As she passed him to grab some refreshments for their guests, his fingers slid down her arm and entwined briefly with hers. The moment of connection reassured her, and for the rest of the evening, as they chatted and played games and finally said good night—with Gavin agreeing to give Carter and Thad a ride back to the mansion so Erin could go straight home to rest—in the back of her mind she knew, they might have been interrupted, but that didn't mean they were through.

What was it Scarlett O'Hara had said? Tomorrow was another day.

CHAPTER
Nine

Carter knew what he was doing when he insisted Gavin take them back to the mansion. Gavin knew he had because of the smile on his face as they walked out to the car. He'd been tempted to punch his friend, but that would lead to questions from Thad, and he wasn't explaining that the boy's father was being a cockblock and therefore deserved to have his block knocked off.

Gavin was an adult. He could wait till tomorrow for sex, right?

Right.

He made it back home, at least. A hot shower and a quick wank meant he actually got some sleep. Waiting till Scarlett was up the next day was a bit harder.

Then he got the text.

Scarlett: I'm going to do a big push this morning to finish the last chapters before Christmas Eve dinner tonight. Want to go together?

Telling himself her work was important—which it was, there was no doubt about that; much more important than his impatient penis—he texted back.

Gavin: Was planning on it! I'll be there at five. Be ready to tell me what you've written.

Scarlett: No pressure!

The string of emojis that came after her words could've meant she was feeling nervous or laughing at him. He wasn't sure which, but if he made her laugh, he'd count that as a bonus. Now he simply had to occupy himself for the rest of the day.

The build site was empty on Christmas Eve. Since he was here, he might as well take an interest in his investment, although he wasn't worried about it in the least. Between Carter and JD, there was no way the resort could fail, so it was pretty much guaranteed money. But having a look around meant that he could at least see what to expect when he came back for visits. JD found him walking through the massive entry, gazing around with appreciation.

"About time you came to take a look."

He shrugged. "Have to know where I'll be living one month out of the year."

JD laughed. "You're more than welcome to stay here for a month or longer. You know that."

He did know. Problem was, he never took off a whole month to be somewhere. He was beginning to feel more and more like he needed to do something to change that.

"Everything all set for the wedding?"

JD led the way toward the west wing of the building. "Oh yeah. Lily is nothing if not efficient. She had everyone whipped into shape weeks ago. Today was a day to pamper herself."

"You two are a good fit." It was a statement, not a question. There was no "seems like" about it; the pair fit together as seamlessly as any couple Gavin had met. He'd seen plenty who had massive cracks from the start—most of his da's marriages were perfect examples—but not JD and Lily. "I like her for you. A lot."

JD grinned. "I can honestly say I've never been happier."

Gavin patted him on the back. "Good. That's what I wanted to know."

They took a look around the space that would be Gimme Two Sugars, as well as Lincoln's yet-to-be-named restaurant. A good bit of the back of house was complete, ready and waiting for machinery and appliances. The east side of the hotel had space for an indoor/outdoor pool that would be completed in the spring, as well as several other leisure and entertainment spaces.

"All rooms are on the upper floors. The suites are coming along nicely. Erin has done a fantastic job keeping us on schedule despite the weather."

"I like her. She's been to New York a couple of times."

"Which is a miracle considering that she's head of construction, but she keeps everyone on such a tight leash that they all managed to actually get time off. She and Lily are similar that way."

"And Claire is the creative of the bunch. The three of you are lucky indeed, JD."

JD beamed. "You don't have to tell me that. Now all we need to do is get you hitched."

For once Gavin didn't remember to protest.

He passed the afternoon finishing up his latest novel from Scarlett, playing some games with Thad and Carter and Linc. As sunset closed in, coming even earlier here in the mountains, he showered and got ready to pick up his date. Anticipation buzzed in his belly, which wouldn't be surprising if it was completely about the missed opportunity for sex, but he found he missed Scarlett's presence more than anything. Having her keep him company, knowing she was nearby even when she was working, the sound of her voice and her laughter. He missed *her*, he realized. Call it odd, considering they had only known each other a few days, but it was true.

And then it was finally time to drive down the mountain.

Scarlett was quick to answer the door after he arrived. "Come on in. I'm not quite ready."

"Take yer time, lass." He certainly took his, eyeing the green velvet dress that hugged her curves, the sexy boots she had on. "Ya look stunnin'."

She ran a brush through her long blonde hair. "Thank you. You're pretty fine yourself, there, Mr. Blackwood."

He glanced down at the black wool trousers and thick hunter-green sweater he wore. "We match." He grinned. "JD warned me ta dress warmly, but he didn't explain why. Any idea what's goin' on?"

She turned to head down the hall, and he followed. "I know the restaurant is the one on top of the mountain at the ski center in Pigeon Forge. We'll ride a sky carriage to get up there. Maybe that's why?"

He watched as she rummaged through a makeup bag, then pulled out mascara. The dark brown color made her eyes stand out even more than they did already. Their pretty green color sparkled as she stared at him in the mirror. "Are you enjoying watching me put on makeup?"

"I enjoy watchin' ya do anythin'," he said, meaning it. "Today was a bit lonely without ya."

Her eyes went wide. "Really?"

"Really."

Scarlett eyed him intently for a few seconds longer, then seemed to collect herself. Closing the mascara, she traded it for her signature red lipstick. "So what did you do to occupy yourself?"

As he outlined his day, Scarlett smoothed on the rich color, put in some earrings that sparkled in the light, and gathered her things. He waited till he had her in the car before asking, "So, the book. What happened?"

She laughed. "You're so impatient."

"I think I've been highly patient, especially since last night. Now tell me."

"Okay, so you know when book one ended, we had the epilogue one year later. In book two, someone has figured out who Levi is, and they're targeting him, putting Abby in danger."

"Uh-huh."

She went through the bare bones of the plot while he drove. A half hour later they met the other couples and Thad, Erin's parents, and Lily's parents at a parking lot on the outskirts of Pigeon Forge. Lily explained that the town had a ski company at the top of the mountain that operated different activities year-round and made snow when the temperatures dropped enough to accommodate it. The only way to get there, however, was the trolley. He could see what looked like cable cars descending the mountain above their heads, and when they stepped into the nearby station, one of the cars waited for them to board.

As they lifted into the air, Scarlett took a seat on one of the benches and stared out into the night. Below them, in the dark, light sparkled as the towns of Pigeon Forge and, farther afield, Gatlinburg spread out below them. "It's always so pretty," Scarlett said. "It doesn't matter the season or whether it's day or night, this view is always gorgeous."

"I agree," Gavin said. But when Scarlett turned her head, he wasn't staring at the view. He was staring at her.

Despite his sincerity, he winked, hoping to lighten the moment for both of them. "It's the truth."

It most certainly was.

Faint pink color bled into Scarlett's cheeks. "Thank you, Gavin."

He wanted to kiss her. He *really* wanted to kiss her, but he was uncertain how she would feel about it in this crowd of her friends. So he waited.

See, he could be patient sometimes. Even if waiting all day was stretching his limits.

The restaurant at the top of the mountain was almost as

beautiful as the Carousel, and the view couldn't be beaten. Dinner was delicious, the wine flowed freely, and the company was more precious than he'd imagined it would be —especially the company sitting in the seat next to him. Gavin couldn't help thinking about how his group of friends had gone from four single men having a dinner at the holidays to this table, full of joy and Christmas spirit. None of it was something he'd expected in his life while growing up, a lonely experience with a bitter mother and occasional holidays hiding in the corner away from jealous stepsiblings. His three friends had been a gift he'd been grateful for, but this... This was an even greater gift, and when he turned his head to watch Scarlett sitting beside him, sparkling like a hundred-carat diamond, he felt a little bit like the Grinch, his heart growing three sizes bigger as he watched her smile and laugh with her friends.

It was dangerous. He couldn't afford to keep letting himself open up. In fact he could hear his mam's voice in the back of his mind: *Don't get yer hopes up.* But what was so wrong with hope? Maybe hope was what they all needed.

And maybe hope was what he had found, here in Black Wolf's Bluff. With Scarlett.

CHAPTER
Ten

A fter dinner, their group traveled back down the mountain and returned to Black Wolf's Bluff, where they stopped at the local nondenominational church for Christmas Eve service. Scarlett didn't attend regularly, but something about a service at the holidays, so many voices raised to sing traditional carols and celebrate joy, always touched her heart. It was a special memory she cherished every year, but this year in particular, with Gavin standing next to her, his strong baritone sounding in her ear, might be the most special yet.

When the service came to a close, they trailed outside to find a line of horse-drawn carriages waiting. JD had the biggest grin on his face. "We don't have snow yet," he declared to the group, emphasizing the *yet*, "although it may start at any moment, but we can still have the fun of a sleigh ride. Pile in, everyone!"

And pile in they did. Somehow Scarlett and Gavin found themselves at the last of the five carriages, the only two waiting to climb in. Gavin bent to whisper in her ear, "Is it possible we might have our very own sleigh ride, just the two of us?"

Her mind immediately went to things best left unthought in a crowd, particularly outside of a church. "Maybe."

He chuckled. "I think I'm gonna enjoy this."

And if he did, she probably would too. No matter what he had in mind.

The driver handed Scarlett aboard. Piles of blankets waited, and Gavin made sure to tuck her in where she would be nice and warm before taking his place beside her—beneath the covers, of course. He put his arm around her shoulders, his heat soaking into her side ensuring she wouldn't get cold anytime soon. In fact, she might be heating up too much.

She tugged the blankets down to give herself some breathing room.

"Everythin' all right?" Gavin asked.

"I'm good." As the carriage set off, she felt a thrill of pleasure go through her and gave a little bounce in the seat. "I can't believe JD arranged this. It's so much fun."

Gavin grinned at her antics. "And just think, until Lily came along, we were sure JD had no' a single romantic bone in his body."

Scarlet grinned up at him. "Sometimes it just takes the right person to bring it out of you."

His gaze fastened on her mouth. "How right ya are, lass."

The carriage picked up speed as they exited the church parking lot, at the end of the line snaking its way toward Main Street. Crisp air nipped at her nose, the temperature dropping in preparation for a snowy Christmas Day according to the forecast, but everywhere else she was toasty warm.

That warmth became hotter when Gavin's palm settled on her stomach. Tingles traveled south from there.

Gavin's breath heated her neck. "Ya know ya tortured me all day."

A secret smile blossomed inside her. She had a feeling he wasn't talking about the torture of waiting to find out the contents of her story, but that didn't mean she would admit the knowledge. Two could play the teasing game.

She settled her hand over his, pressing him closer, savoring his touch. "I wrote as fast as I could."

He growled in her ear. "It's no' about how fast ya write."

"Then what is it about?" she asked as innocently as she could.

"It's about where ya were."

"Where was I?"

"Away from me."

She tipped her head up to look at him, bringing her free hand up to cup his stubbled cheek. The texture tempted her, and she rubbed her thumb over it. "I missed you too."

He grinned. "I know."

She backhanded his belly. "That's a terrible response."

"What? Why is it terrible?"

The fact that he was laughing made her mouth twitch, but she controlled her amusement—barely. "It's like romance movies where the hero always says, 'I know' or 'ditto.'" She didn't mention what the words were in response to. She didn't expect Gavin to say he loved her, but he was the one who'd opened the can of worms. "So rude."

He captured her hand and brought it up to his lips, kissing her mitten-covered fingers. "No' in this case. I really did know. After last night, how could I no'." He arched a brow, a twinkle appearing in his eyes.

Of course he knew. She wondered if he'd taken care of himself the way she'd taken of things after everyone had left. Pressing his hand harder against her stomach to still the butterflies taking flight there, she admitted, "We *were* rudely interrupted."

And though she'd missed more than just sex—she had missed him, which was odd considering they'd known each other, what, four days?—something held her back from saying so. That voice of caution that kept reminding her that he would soon be gone. She was afraid she'd miss a lot more than his body when that happened. It didn't matter how much she told herself not to; she liked Gavin. She could do a lot more than like him, she suspected. She might resign herself to taking what she could get—and enjoying every minute—but a huge part of her would be sad when he left.

"We're in the middle of town," she pointed out as Main Street breezed by. "It's not like you can do anything about it here."

"I can't?" His smile shot a thrill down her spine. "Ya underestimate me."

Please show me how I've underestimated you. She pressed her lips tightly together.

When Gavin's hand moved beneath hers, she startled. Up up up until it rested just below her breast. Surely she had too many layers on to be hot and bothered by the simple place-ment of his hand, but apparently not. She squirmed.

Gavin's smiling lips descended to touch hers. "Don't worry, you won't have to wait too long."

God, she hoped not.

He palmed her breast. Could he feel her heart slamming into her rib cage? Because she knew, even if they began fore-play here, it wasn't stopping until they'd gone all the way tonight. And the way she felt right now, all the way would mean a choir of heavenly angels singing hallelujah—hope-fully more than once.

The slow back-and-forth of his fingers tightened her nipple even through her clothes. "Gavin," she whimpered against his lips.

He hummed. "Problem?"

"Just that you're moving too slow."

"We've got all the time in the world." He nipped her bottom lip. "Or at least until I can take you home and do this right."

Despite his words, his finger slipped to the low vee of her

bodice, then tucked beneath it. Delved beneath the edge of her bra. Bare fingers found her nipple and began a slow roll that nearly had her crying out.

"That's it, kitten," Gavin told her. "Purr for me."

Her body went wet.

Gavin teased her breast for long minutes, punctuating each one with a kiss that left her longing for more. She had no idea where they were, if they were still in town or heading back toward the church. She didn't care. She only cared that the torture continued.

And it needed to be mutual.

Turning her hand, she pressed her palm against Gavin's erect length.

"Scarlett."

Yes, that strain was exactly how she felt. "What?"

She rubbed a single finger up, then down. Gavin choked. His hand retreated to hold hers still.

Scarlett pouted. She didn't think she'd ever pouted in her life, but she did now. "Hey."

Gavin dropped his chin, taking deep breaths. "If that hand moves again, we may have ta stop altogether."

"Why?"

"Because I might make a mess in my pants if we don'."

Before she could respond, the carriage rocked to a halt. Glancing up, she saw that they were outside her house. "Delivery service?"

"Thank God," Gavin said.

He had her out of the carriage and had tipped the driver within half a minute. With a sharp wave, he dragged her toward the door. She'd have laughed if she didn't feel equally as urgent about things.

Inside, she locked the door, turned, and found Gavin tearing off his outer layers. "This first time might be fast," he said, fingers fumbling the buttons of his shirt.

"Not too fast, I hope." She joined him in stripping.

"I haven't worried about bein' too fast since secondary school behind the gymnasium, but ya do something to me, lass."

She nearly preened. She did preen when she slipped her dress from her shoulders, allowing the heavy material to slide down her skin, revealing the silky emerald lace bra she wore. The matching panties and garter belt came next, then silk hosiery. Gavin hissed.

"Those better come off," he warned, nodding toward her legs. "I don' want to tear them."

A shiver went through her, but she made an equal show of removing the delicate silk, easing it down each leg before doing the same with the garter belt. When that cleared her feet, Gavin allowed a rough curse free and gripped her hand. They were heading for her bedroom so fast the walls actually spun.

Christmas lights twinkled outside her bedroom window, illuminating the way as they crossed to her bed. Gavin threw the covers back before laying her out for him to admire.

"Such a bonnie lass ya are, Scarlett. My sweetheart." He traced a finger from the center of her throat, between her breasts, down her stomach to the edge of her panties. "Let me have these."

She lifted her hips, allowing him to pull the cloth down her legs. Her breasts shimmied with the movement, her heart racing, her stomach fluttering with anticipation, and between her legs…God, she was so wet. So needy. Come to think of it, it might not be Gavin who went too fast.

In the near darkness, Gavin straightened next to the bed and shoved down his boxers. Soft white light illuminated the ridges of his muscles, the wide shoulders and chest, the heavy thighs. And between those thighs… She reached for him.

He grinned at her greed but didn't deny her. Instead he crawled onto the bed on all fours, giving her complete access. When she wrapped her hand around his cock, he groaned loud and long. "Aye, just like that," he whispered, voice like gravel. "Don' be shy now. I'm wantin' ya just as bad."

And to prove it, he centered himself over her and pulled the cups of her bra down, not even bothering with the clasp. When one nipple popped free, his mouth was there, drawing her in, taking as much as he could get with each hard suck. Scarlett arched with a cry, desperate to give him more. He made quick work of the other side, then moved between them, giving her breasts equal treatment that drove her nearly to the edge.

She dragged her fingernails lightly up the rigid length of his cock. "Gavin, please."

His teeth scraped her nipple. Her core clenched hard.

"Please, now." She didn't want to orgasm without him inside her. "I need it."

Raising his head, he looked hard at her before nodding. A quick glance over the side of the bed drew a curse.

"What is it?"

Gavin hopped up and sprinted for the door. "Be right back."

She had no more than a minute to wonder what he was after before he returned, a foil packet between his fingers. She grinned. "Forgot something, did you?"

"Luckily no' fer long." He tore open the foil and wrapped the condom carefully down his beautiful cock. When he climbed back onto the bed, she had her arms open for him.

"Bet one of yer heroes never forgot the rubbers," he muttered against her breast. Teeth scraped her nipple gently, and then he was back to sucking.

"Lots of things don't happen in romance novels," she admitted distractedly. "Doesn't ruin the real thing." Because the real thing was pretty damn fantastic.

Gavin laid his weight down on her, and everything inside her went still, absorbing the feel of him, glorying in his weight. She wrapped her arms around his back and pulled him even closer. Gavin switched to her opposite breast, and she surged up beneath him, a thrill shaking her when he barely moved.

"Gavin." Her fingernails scraped against the skin of his back, and she trailed them down, down, down until she could palm the firm globes of his ass. Her legs parted instinctively, letting him in. "Gavin."

He knew what she needed. Curving his back, he slid his cock between her legs. She brought her knees up, her heels urging him forward.

He raised his head. "All right?"

"God yes."

He grinned even as his cock pushed forward, parting her, making way for himself deep inside her body. When he hilted, she reached down, feeling the place where he'd entered her, feeling where he ended and she began. Her hips tilted without thought. "More."

Gavin cursed. Holding himself up on one elbow, he began a heavy in-and-out motion while he teased her breast, petting, tweaking, massaging. Watching his eyes devour the sight of her was almost too much, and she closed her eyes, focusing on the sharp surge of desire as her body shouted with delight.

"Not long," she said, straining. She forced herself to meet Gavin's eyes, to share that too-intimate moment as her body clenched hard on his fierce invasion, then flew free. "Gavin!"

He held her gaze, refusing to let go until her orgasm waned. A few minutes of petting, of heavy breathing, and he came up to his knees. His big hands caught her behind her legs and pushed her thighs back toward her body. The move angled her hips, opening her to receive him even deeper. The rhythm he started up had her crying out immediately.

"Come on, lass, come on," he urged. "I want another one."

He hadn't had his first. "I can't—"

"Ya can and ya will, Scarlet. Give me what I want. Come on now." He hammered into her, quickening his thrusts. Scarlett grabbed hold of her thighs and threw her head back, barely able to breathe, feeling the rise of that pleasure all over again.

Gavin reached for one of her hands, lifted it, and placed her fingers on her clit. The delicate nub was hard, straining outside its hood. "Touch yerself, Scarlett. I want to see how beautiful ya are when ya explode." A couple more thrusts had him grunting, a grimace taking over that full mouth, and strain constricted his words. "I'm gonna come. Come with me, darlin'."

"I— I am—" Her fingers circled her clit, pressing harder, shooting a live wire of pleasure through her body. "Gavin, I—"

"That's it. That's it," he coached.

Her spine curled. "Gavin, I'm coming. I'm coming!"

A flurry of thrusts pounded her pelvis, setting off a fire that threatened to consume her. Her body clamped down on his, tight, tighter, her focus narrowing to her core…

And then she was there. She was over.

"Aye!" Gavin shouted. "That's my girl."

Long moments later she collapsed back onto the bed, breath like a runaway freight train. Gavin's weight between her legs disappeared, and she heard the bathroom door open. Getting rid of the condom. Next thing she was aware of was his body stretching out next to her. "Now you can sleep," he said in her ear. His hand settled on her mound, petting her gently. "Sleep for a little while. I'll wake you soon."

She couldn't wait.

A kiss brushed her cheek, her lips, before he sighed and curled around her. "Merry Christmas, lass."

CHAPTER
Eleven

S carlett stirred as Gavin trailed his fingers over her breast. Pleasure and pain zinged through her body. She pushed his hand away. "I'm sore, you lech."

Gavin's laugh reached her slowly waking ears. "Ye're sore? I'm sore."

She gestured in the general direction of his crotch without opening her eyes. "That's what you get for using that thing so much."

What she said registered just as the words left her mouth, and she squeezed her eyes shut, heat rushing into her cheeks. Oh God, had she really told Gavin he'd used his penis too much? She really couldn't be trusted to talk like a responsible adult when she was still half asleep. With a groan she hoped he attributed to lack of sleep and not embarrassment, she rolled over and pulled the covers over her head.

They were slowly pulled back until light hit her eyes. Gavin's mouth touched her ear. "You enjoyed me usin' that thing, lass. Don' try to deny it."

She covered her face with her hands even as a giggle escaped. Fingers landed on her ribs, and Gavin gave her a light tickle.

"No no no!" She laughed as she rolled over to face him. Pointing a demanding finger in his direction, she commanded, "No tickling."

Gavin ignored the finger and leaned in for a kiss. She slapped a hand over her mouth. "Mownin' bweath!"

He grinned. "I used yer mouthwash."

"I didn't!"

A warning light filled his eyes, and the next thing she knew she was on her back, Gavin's mouth landing kisses over her neck and chest and shoulders and face. He saved her mouth for last, but he limited himself to a close-mouthed kiss before backing away. Satisfaction filled his eyes when he took in her flushed, laughing face.

Then, "Right. Coffee?"

She nodded. "Please."

She watched as he left the room, devouring the sight of his bare chest and back and long, bare legs beneath his boxers. God, he was sexy. And last night had been…mind-blowing. That was the only word that could come close to describing it. Totally mind-blowing.

And now that sexy man was in her kitchen making coffee.

She couldn't scramble out of the bed fast enough.

Five minutes later she hobbled into the kitchen, mouth fresh, legs aching. "Am I walking bowlegged? I feel like I'm walking bowlegged. Heroines never walk like this. They take all the sex they can get and keep on going. I, on the other hand, definitely feel like I was riding a horse all night."

"You were ridin' somethin'." Gavin wiggled his eyebrows at her.

Laughter bubbled up. "Bad pun! So bad." She shuffled toward him.

"But it made ya laugh." He came to her side. "Heroines don' have mornin' breath either," he pointed out, "but here we are, stuck in reality." Scooping her into his arms, he deposited her onto the counter before she could blink. When her thighs split open around his hips, she hissed.

Gavin gave her a look of sympathy. "Poor babe." He gripped her thighs with his big hands and began to massage the aching muscles. "How's that?"

She grimaced. "Guess I'm a bit out of practice." *And old*, she told herself. *Don't forget old.*

He ducked his head to meet her eyes. "I'm no' complainin'."

Considering how often he'd woken her—and she'd woken him—during the rather active night, she guessed not. As he kneaded her aching muscles, tenderness welled up. She reached for him then, unable to wait a second more. The scruff on his cheeks was longer, softer than it had been against her inner thighs last night. Cupping his cheeks, she raised his head and met his lips with her own.

A groan escaped him, making her smile. His reactions were so masculine, so rough where his manners were so smooth. A wealth of contradictions in one body that came together to create one compelling package she couldn't get enough of.

Gavin took a deep breath, pulled back, and smiled down at her. "That's what I wanted for Christmas mornin'."

She'd forgotten it was Christmas morning. "Sorry."

"Stop apologizin'." He raised his eyebrows. "Last night was more physically demandin' of you than it was of me." He leaned in, kissed her again, and set his forehead against hers. "And I enjoyed every second of it."

"Me too."

While she continued to sit on the counter, Gavin rummaged through her cupboards, found a couple of coffee cups, and poured them coffee. After doctoring one according to her instructions, he handed her a light, sweet cup of coffee while drinking his black. The idea made her shudder.

"So…" She hid her uncertainty behind her coffee mug,

focusing on the liquid instead of Gavin's face. "I have a Christmas gift for you under the tree."

"Is that right?"

"It is." She dared to look up. Excitement filled his eyes. He looked like a kid who had been let loose in a candy store. "Would you like to open it?"

"Sure would." He hesitated. "I have a gift for you as well, but it's in my car."

She laughed. "I completely forgot about the car last night. I guess we can retrieve it later."

He took her coffee cup and assisted her down from the countertop. As they walked into the living room, Scarlett caught her breath at the sight that waited outside the windows. White blanketed the world—a layer of snow, pristine and beautiful. She went immediately to the window. "Look at that. A white Christmas!"

Gavin moved behind her. His chest met her back as his arms came around her waist, his chin settling on her shoulder. "Beautiful, aye?"

"It is." She frowned. "I hope it doesn't keep people from coming to the wedding."

"JD told me he had the road salted yesterday, so the mountain is safe. Judgin' from the asphalt out there, I think the roads in town will be fine."

He was right, the road outside her house was mostly clear. The main worry would be the mountain, and if that was taken care of… "Good. I wouldn't want anything to put a damper on their day."

Gavin tucked his face against her neck. His stubble brushed along the sensitive skin there. When she tipped her head to the side to give him access, he placed a light kiss just below her ear, right on her throbbing pulse. His chuckle blew warm air against her skin. "Can't leave a love bite on the bridesmaid. That would be embarrassin'."

She grinned over her shoulder. "I definitely wouldn't want to explain that."

He grinned back. "I imagine we'll have some explainin' to do when we get up the mountain anyway."

He was probably right. Not that she minded.

"So…" He nipped the lobe of her ear. "Did ya say somethin' about a gift?"

He sounded like a little boy excited over a toy. It reminded her of how he looked when he slept, as if all the cares of the world had fallen away and the charm and enthusiasm that was pure Gavin was suddenly free. "I think I did mention something about a gift."

Leading him over to the Christmas tree, she pulled him down to sit in front of it, face-to-face with her. Beneath the lit branches lay a box wrapped in shimmery gold paper, a big bow on top. Hesitation filled her. Gavin was literally the man who could have anything, and what she'd gotten him was small. Would he like it?

She handed the box over. "Merry Christmas, Gavin."

There was no careful unwrapping of the paper for her Scotsman; no, he tore into it immediately, shredding the paper in his eagerness to get to the box. Her worry dissipated; all she could do was grin as she watched him eagerly reveal his surprise.

Gavin opened the box flaps. A mound of tissue paper lay below. "What is this?" Grasping the material, he pulled until he was surrounded by a sea of white. Inside was a thick stack of paper bound with a rubber band.

"I thought you could use something to read on your way home," she explained.

He lifted the packet from the box, mouth open in awe. "This is your manuscript, Scarlett."

"It is. Aside from my editor, you'll be the first to read it. I know I already told you—"

He tackled her, taking her backward until her spine met

the rug and he was lying on top of her. "It's perfect." His warm lips met hers, pushed them open, and his tongue delved inside. She savored the taste of him, the eagerness of his mouth, the soft surge of his desire against her thigh. When he lifted his head, she was hot and flustered. "I can't wait to read it."

Happiness lit inside her. "I figured you'd need a reminder of that quirky author you discovered in an unusual way on your trip to the Tennessee mountains."

"I appreciate the reminder"—he ducked his head to nibble her collarbone—"but I don' think I'll be in danger of forgettin'."

Her breath caught, but Gavin didn't give her a chance to reply. Instead he kissed her again, and for a long while after that, thinking was impossible.

Around lunchtime they headed up the mountain to get ready for the wedding. At the base of the stairs, they parted, her to go up to Lily's suite, Gavin to wherever the guys were, but not without a kiss. Her lips tingled as she mounted the stairs and walked to the room where Lily was getting ready. When she entered, Erin and Claire were already there.

"About time!" Erin reached for a hug. "We thought you were never gonna get here."

"Not that we blame you," Claire said. "Who would want to leave that hunk behind?"

Scarlett blushed.

Erin giggled. "That's it, you owe me five bucks," she told Claire.

"I told you guys things were heating up," Lily said, exiting the bathroom.

Scarlett turned, eyeing Lily in her white silk robe. Her makeup was perfection, her blonde curls that she'd let grow out a bit falling over her shoulders in beautiful disarray. Ignoring the comments about Gavin, she said, "You look beautiful."

Lily nodded toward Claire. "Thank God we have an artist among us. No way could I get a hairstylist and makeup artist up here on the mountain on Christmas Day."

Claire waved her arms over Lily as if showing off a painting. "It's not hard to do when you have such a good canvas."

"Are you nervous, Lily?" Scarlett asked.

Lily's grin held the light of a thousand candles. "Not in the slightest. One of the big advantages of doing this at my age instead of twenty years ago, in my opinion."

"Definitely," Claire said. "I threw up the morning of my wedding to Jared. And had the added pressure of being a virgin."

"Ugh." Erin groaned. "That would've made it even worse. I'd been with Stephen all through high school and was still so, so nervous on my wedding day."

"I have zero doubts that this is the right thing to do," Lily said. "I don't think I've ever been as comfortable with anyone as I was with JD from the moment we met." A sheen of tears appeared in her eyes. "He's my best friend."

"Don't go crying!" Claire said, rushing over with a tissue in her hand. "You'll ruin your makeup."

Laughter filled the room. Scarlett watched her friend, thinking about how similar they were—neither of them had married in their younger years; both of them had long-term careers, but no children. Both were content with those areas of their life, even if their romantic lives had been lacking when they met the person they wanted to be with.

When *Lily* met the person she wanted to be with, of course. Lily. Not Scarlett.

And yet she couldn't help thinking that this morning had felt completely natural, that her time with Gavin had been the smoothest she'd ever experienced in a romantic relationship. But this was temporary, right? He would leave for Scotland tomorrow, and she would be here in Black Wolf's Bluff, writing her stories, living her life. She could be content doing that forever.

So why did her chest ache at the thought of Gavin leaving?

The three bridesmaids worked on their makeup together, fixed each other's hair, and donned their dresses before turning their attention to Lily's wedding gown. Knowing they would be outside in December, Lily had chosen a strapless dress that fitted her body all the way down to her thighs, where it flared out into a ball gown. The top would be covered during the ceremony with a faux fur coat of creamy white, keeping her warm and beautiful in the chill air.

Once Lily was ready, they sneaked out into the yard for pictures. Sooo many pictures. The photographer shooed the bridesmaids away when they were done, and led JD out for the first look at his bride. Though it was a private moment, Claire and Erin and Scarlett looked on from the upstairs window, and there was definitely some makeup repair that had to take place after that.

More pictures followed, with the groomsmen coming out in their black tuxes, smart and sexy, to pair with the bridesmaids. Gavin in a tux was devastatingly handsome. The flutter in her belly when she saw him, his curls falling over his forehead, his grin, flirty and focused only on her, had her thinking back to those moments watching Lily upstairs. What if she and Gavin weren't short-term? What if there might be more for them just as there had been for each of her friends? Was it even possible?

And just like before, she shoved the thoughts away. Now was the time to focus on Lily and JD. Their wedding. Their future. She could think about herself—and Gavin—later.

CHAPTER
Twelve

L ily was beautiful. JD's gaze came to rest on her at the end of the aisle, and Gavin could tell instantly that this moment in time would be a perfect memory for both of them. No fear. No worry. No shallow lust that wouldn't last the week. Just a deep, abiding love and desire that shone from their eyes in a way he'd never seen before.

When tears welled up in JD's eyes, Gavin knew he was right.

Linc laid a hand on JD's shoulder, his firm grip steadying their friend. In front of Gavin, Carter surreptitiously swiped a hand over his face. Across the aisle from them, where the bridesmaids were lined up, Gavin could see Claire dabbing at her eyes. Erin beamed, watching her friend walk slowly down the aisle. But when Gavin's eyes reached Scarlett, she wasn't looking at JD, and she wasn't looking at Lily.

She was looking at him.

That look hit him full in the chest.

He wasn't certain he could say why. He only knew that he couldn't push it from his mind—it had been something soft, cautious, but happy. Something yearning. Something… He didn't want to use the word *love* because they hadn't known each other long enough for love, but almost like the precursor. Satisfaction and joy and friendship, all rolled into a single look.

Maybe that's why he couldn't describe it, because it was too many things at once. Too many things that made his chest feel funny. And at the same time, too many things that felt just right.

After a short discussion of the joys of a wedding on a white Christmas day, the judge performing the ceremony led Lily and JD in their vows, then in the exchange of rings. A Christmas hymn came next, then a prayer. When JD kissed his bride, the room erupted, only to quiet down when the judge asked the couple to turn and face the audience. Holding hands, JD and Lily turned, and the biggest smiles that Gavin thought he'd ever seen broke out across their faces.

"May I present to you, Mr. and Mrs. John David and Lillian Ann Lane."

The crowd stood, everyone clapping, as Lily and JD made their way back down the aisle. At the end they disappeared into the house for their first moments together as a newly married couple, alone. Gavin thought they better enjoy it, given the enthusiasm of the crowd. They might not have a moment to themselves once they came back out.

Lincoln stepped up to the podium and directed the well-wishers into the next tent over for "a feast to be remembered," and then he took Claire's hand and walked her back down the aisle. Carter approached Erin, and hands clasped, they followed.

And then it was his turn. Gavin stepped forward, gaze locked on Scarlett, and reached for her hand. She stepped forward, her velvet gown swishing and swaying with her steps, and reached for him. When their fingers touched, a surge of pleasure shot up his arm. Pleasure and satisfaction. Joy and friendship. All the things he'd seen in Scarlett's eyes, surging through his heart as he entwined his fingers with hers.

For a moment he froze, captivated by that feeling. Scarlett smiled up at him, green eyes dazzling. "Amazing," he said.

She blushed.

They made their way to the back of the tent and into the house to meet Lincoln and Carter, Claire and Erin. His friends were cuddling their partners, warming them up. When Gavin and Claire entered, Carter held up his hand. "Before we get bombarded—and before Lily and JD come back from wherever they are—"

"Probably making out somewhere," Linc suggested.

Carter chuckled, shaking his head. "Can you blame him?"

"Not a bit," Linc declared smugly. "I intend to follow his example soon enough."

Claire backhanded his arm.

Carter ignored the byplay. "We have an announcement."

"We?" Gavin asked.

"We." Carter looked at Erin, warmth and something infinitely gentle welling in his eyes. Bringing their clasped hands up to his mouth, he kissed her knuckles. "We're pregnant."

"What?" Lincoln shouted. Excited exclamations filled the room, laughter welling as hugs and congratulations and questions were exchanged. Erin admitted they'd waited to tell Thad until they were certain everything was all right, and if Thad didn't know, they didn't want anyone else slipping.

"A wedding and a baby. Who would've thought y'all were all such fast workers?" Claire drawled, eyeing Carter.

"Does that mean we need ta expect an announcement from the two of ya soon?" Gavin asked. Scarlett got the impression he was only semi-joking.

"No babies," Claire said, her voice firm. "I'm too old for babies."

Lincoln hugged her to his side. "We will work on the rest of the list later."

Scarlett snickered. "Better work hard; it doesn't sound like she's too enthusiastic, Lincoln."

The rest of the group took up the teasing until JD and Lily appeared from down the hall. Lily looked slightly mussed but no worse for wear.

"You guys ready to celebrate?" Lily asked.

"We are," Carter said. He nodded his head toward the rest of the group. "We let them in on our secret."

"Finally!" Lily said.

"Wait, you knew?" Claire asked.

"She knew before anyone else," Erin admitted. "Almost before me."

The story of how Erin had found out she was pregnant and told Carter was relayed as they moved into the reception space. Lily and JD were commandeered by the crowd, as expected, and Lincoln and Claire went to direct the food.

"I think we deserve a drink," Carter said.

"Ginger ale for me," Erin requested.

A quick trip to the bar and they were back. Scarlett and Erin had commandeered a table near the edge of the dance floor, though the music hadn't started yet. "This morning sickness has been kicking my ass," Erin was saying.

"Carter told me you were sick before we came," Gavin put in. "Is everythin' all right?"

"Doc claims it's nothing to worry about." She ran a hand down her stomach. "He is sending me to a specialist, but that's a precaution. Apparently I have a 'geriatric pregnancy.'" She grimaced.

Scarlett joined her. "Of course they couldn't have a better term for it."

"Right?"

"I told Doc if we were 'geriatric' we wouldn't have had the energy to get in this condition," Carter joked.

Just as their laughter died down, Iris stopped at the table. "Could I sit with y'all?"

"Of course." Carter pulled out a chair for their friend, took her drink order, and disappeared into the crowd.

"You look gorgeous," Scarlett told Iris. "That peacock blue is phenomenal on you."

Scarlett was right. The librarian looked smashing in her velvet dress. Scarlett had explained after their time at the library that her friend had recently separated from a rather stodgy husband and had taken to wearing bright, flattering colors that looked great with her naturally gray hair. She hadn't gone wrong today.

"Thank you. I love that Lily chose cream for you all. A wedding of winter white. And even the weather cooperated."

Carter returned from the bar with Iris's drink.

"It's nice to see Lily so happy," Iris said.

"She is," Erin said. "I haven't gotten to see you in a while between work and stuff. How are things going with you?"

Iris frowned. "Kirk is making sure they're not going well at all."

Gavin gathered that was the soon-to-be ex when Scarlett added, "That man is such an asshole."

Iris took a long sip of her drink. "He definitely is." She brightened. "But enough about me."

Scarlett laughed. "It's okay to talk about you, Iris."

Her friend shook her head. "I want to think about happy things today."

Gavin thought he knew a way to help with that. "Ladies, how about we go over to the photo stand and I take your picture?"

The photo stand was a vintage car parked in the snow with a Christmas wreath on the windshield. The ladies piled into the back seat, bundled together, and smiled for the camera as he took shots from different angles and flattered them mercilessly—every word of which was true. And he loved that Scarlett didn't get jealous, just laughed along with her friends and soaked up the fun. When they stepped out, Erin insisted on taking Gavin and Scarlett's picture together. He brushed the snow from the hood of the vehicle, took Scarlett by the waist, and lifted her to the surface. "Perfect." When he kissed her, Scarlett opened her mouth, moaning a little as his tongue met hers.

The sound of Erin's phone clicking reached his ears. "Nice one, Gavin!"

Breaking away from Scarlett, he gave Erin a wink. "I'm never content with just the one," and he proceeded to bombard Scarlett with kisses while Erin laughed and took numerous photos.

"You are such a flirt," Scarlett told him when he finally let her down, flushed and blushing from their play.

"And ya love it," he pointed out.

"I'd never admit to that," she teased. "You're arrogant enough as it is."

He pretended to be wounded, hand placed dramatically on his heart, then hustled her onto the dance floor.

An extravagant dinner followed, and Claire's desserts won amazing accolades. The wedding cake was chocolate, iced in white with candy evergreen trees and sugared cranberries to decorate. Beautiful as well as decadent—Gavin had never seen anything like it.

Night had fallen when Lily and JD interrupted the dancing to announce their departure. No throwing garters for Lily, which JD had told him was an old-fashioned tradition here in the States. She did toss a small bouquet that landed as if on purpose in Iris's hands. Scarlett's friend blushed as many of the younger single men sauntered over afterward.

At least they had good sense.

The crowd followed the bride and groom to the front of the mansion where their SUV awaited. Gavin put a hand on Scarlett's elbow to hold her back for a moment.

"Is everything okay?" she asked.

"O' course." He smiled, reaching up to push a hanging curl back behind her ear. Why did he feel nervous all of a sudden. "It was a beautiful weddin'."

"The best."

Enough about them. He cleared his throat. "I like seein' ya so happy, lass."

Her eyes went wide, staring into his. "Thank you." She brought a hand up, rubbing against the stubble that he could never keep permanently gone.

He put his hand over hers, holding her close. "Stay with me tonight?"

"I'd like that."

Just that—no equivocation or hesitance. Scarlett wanted something and wasn't afraid to tell him so.

He couldn't help but kiss her, crowd wandering around or not. He didn't care who saw them, only that his lips were on hers. It might be the best kiss he'd ever had, because as he delved into her mouth, he realized what he tasted wasn't only Scarlett. It was hope. He wanted that hope, had been missing it in his life for longer than he'd known. And now here it was, standing in his arms.

He wouldn't ignore it. If he could keep this woman in his life for longer than one week, he would do it. One week or ten, even one hundred, it didn't matter. He wanted more time with her. He wanted to find out where this feeling would lead. And he would start tonight.

CHAPTER
Thirteen

B y the time they closed the door behind them that night, Scarlett's feet were aching more than her legs had that morning. "I don't think I've ever eaten that much at a wedding, but I also don't think I've ever worked off that much food at a wedding. That dance floor was insane." She flopped back on the bed, raised one foot, and attempted to unbuckle the dress shoe she'd worn since noon.

Gavin came to stand in front of her, grin in place. He took her foot in his hands and finished the job, tossed the shoe over his shoulder to Lord knew where, then held his hand out. "Gimme."

She lifted her other foot.

After he removed that shoe—and tossed it—he crawled onto the bed next to her and flopped down to stretch out on his back. "I know what you mean. Lincoln added ten pounds to my waistline, and the dance floor took it away."

"And those desserts." Scarlett groaned. "Claire did such a good job."

"That cake…" Gavin said.

"The crème brûlée…" Scarlet said.

A laugh rumbled through Gavin's chest. "We'd best just

agree that the whole thing was fantastic or we'll go through the entire menu."

He had a point.

Gathering what energy she had left, she hiked up the long skirt of her bridesmaid's dress, got to her knees, and wobbled over to straddle Gavin. He smiled up at her, his lopsided grin tugging at her heart. Bending down, she kissed that grin away.

"Mmm." He returned the gesture with enthusiasm, his hands going to her hips to hold her in place. "That was nice."

"I may need a nap before we go any further." She couldn't help laughing. "It's times like these that I feel my age."

"What do ya mean? We're in the prime of our lives, darlin'." He began a soothing rub up and down her thighs that did more than soothe—it shot tingles through her lower body that might have a shot at waking her up a bit if he kept going.

She sat down on his thighs, centering herself above a particularly interesting part of his anatomy, and raised her hands over her shoulders to fish for the zipper to her dress.

Gavin narrowed his eyes. She watched them brighten to light amber as her movements gently rocked her over his cock. One hand rose to her cheek, his thumb rubbing along the soft skin there. "I love the pink that rises in yer cheeks every time ya get aroused."

She barked out a laugh at his frank words. "I guess I'm just not used to such a forthright man friend."

"Man friend." He frowned. "I'm not sure how I feel about that description. Man friend." He said the words as if testing them.

"Any other suggestions?"

Gavin opened his mouth, closed it, opened it again. "My brain is too tired to come up with one."

"Gavin Blackwood, speechless?"

"Not speechless, just…" He ran his hands up her thighs

again, this time taking her skirt with them. "Aye, okay, speechless."

Having wrangled her zipper sufficiently down, Scarlett pulled the sides open in the back and began removing the sleeves. "I don't blame you. It's been a long day."

He reached up, tugging the material down her neck, over her breasts, down to her waist. "But a bonnie one." Fingertips began to trace circles over her skin.

She closed her eyes, tipping her head back to enjoy the sensation of Gavin's fingers on her body. A sigh escaped.

"How about a bath?" Gavin asked.

"In the massive tub?" She opened her eyes and grinned down at him. "The one where you first read my book? Then showed up and demanded I fill you in on the rest of the story?"

He spread his hands wide. "And look how that turned out."

She tipped herself to the side. "How can I resist that invitation?"

The tub truly was massive. As she stripped her dress off, Gavin turned the water on, leaving it to run while he undressed. She was a bit sad to see the tux go—he'd been so sexy in it, like an old-fashioned Bond figure—but seeing him without it was better. Gavin naked was nothing short of a masterpiece. As his shirt came off, she admired the width of his heavy shoulders, the narrow strip of dark hair that ran down his chest, his belly, and farther, into his slacks. He unbuckled his belt, slid his pants down, and she got to drool over his long legs covered in short black hair. He was the epitome of masculine like this, stripped down, primal. She thought she could probably stare at him forever.

Gavin got down to his boxers and moved over to test the water before crossing the bathroom to where she waited. "Turn around."

She turned. Gavin released the clasp on her bra, allowing it to slide down her arms without help as he kept her breasts in his hands. There was something about the relief of that weight that had her sagging back against him. His fingers began to lightly play with her nipples. The sensation made her core clench.

"I get the feeling you're a breast man, Gavin."

"What gave ya that idea?"

She could actually hear the grin in his words. "The fact that you can't keep your hands off my boobs?"

He tucked his head down beside hers. "I told ya, all of us boys dream of booby traps."

Laughter bubbled up like it always did when she was with him. She'd heard women say the most important trait in a partner was a sense of humor, but she'd never experienced it before. She didn't consider herself funny either, but something about Gavin's humor seemed to bring it out in her too. It felt good—the laughter, the smiles, the easy way they got along. Gavin wasn't afraid to be serious, but neither was he constantly throwing out angst or drama just for the "fun" of it. It was restful, being with him. She was going to miss it.

"I think I'm goin' to miss ya too," Gavin said in her ear.

Had she spoken that out loud? For a moment she was mortified, that hot flush covering her cheeks for a reason other than arousal, but then his words registered. Besides, he'd said before that he missed her; why should she be embarrassed about it now?

"I'm kind of glad I'm not the only one," she admitted.

"No, ye're no'." Gavin released her breasts and stepped back, but his hand clasped hers as he moved toward the tub. Kneeling, he dragged her panties down her legs. "Come on, get in."

He went first, lying back against one end, his legs in a vee to make room for her. She settled between them, luxuriating in the deep heat of the water as she leaned back against his chest. It felt so good on her tired muscles.

Gavin's arms came around her again, crossing over her stomach to pull her back tighter against him. "Holdin' ya feels so right, lass."

She agreed. "It does, doesn't it?"

They lay in silence for a long while, Scarlett enjoying the heat, enjoying just being in Gavin's arms. As the time passed, she could feel his cock firming beneath her, but he didn't push for anything further, simply enjoyed the moment with her.

"So…" he said finally.

She stirred from her stupor, her ears perking up. "So…?"

"So I leave in the mornin'."

Her heart felt like it sank to the bottom of the tub. "I know."

His chin rubbed against her head as he talked. "I can' remember the last Christmas I enjoyed this much."

"Me too," she whispered. Although she visited her friends on Christmas Day, she hadn't spent Christmas Eve or Christmas morning with anyone in so long she'd almost forgotten what it was like. And to spend it with Gavin? That had been particularly special. She could be happy on her own, but she was even happier when she was with him.

"I don' remember if I told ya, but my da's been married six times."

Shock rippled through her. "Whoa."

"Aye." His hand drifted up and down her belly, swishing the water around. "I grew up with him in and out of marriages, his new wives battlin' with the old ones, my mam upset with everyone around her, including me, because her life hadn't turned out how she wanted it to be. Then stepsiblings started comin', and that only made it worse. It was no' a grand situation."

She brought her hands up to his thighs, stroking along the rough hair there to comfort him. "I imagine not."

"I've had a rule for myself, pretty much my entire adult life, that I would no' date a woman for more than a week."

That was a surprise, and not a welcome one. Here she'd been imagining that maybe, *maybe* he might want to see her again. Maybe something deeper might be growing. She didn't expect him to marry her after a week, but she felt a connection with Gavin that she hadn't with any other man, ever.

"See, my da was always runnin' off with the next woman he fell into bed with, thinkin' he was in love, and then marryin' her, only to divorce her six months or a year or eighteen months later. He made my life so unstable that I never wanted to put anyone else through that, includin' myself. But with you…"

He'd said *but. But* was a good thing, right? Her fingers clenched on his thighs.

Gavin sighed. "With you, Scarlett, I feel somethin' I've never felt before. I could never rush out and get married like my da did, but there's somethin' about you… I really want—"

Was he saying…?

"I really want to spend more time with ya."

Her heart began a rapid tattoo behind her breastbone.

"Would ya consider comin' to see Scotland? I can take ya to all the sites, show ya around." His hand flattened on her belly, pressed down. "Most of all, I just want to see ya again."

She couldn't take it anymore. Rising up, she turned on her knees to face him. "I want that too. I wanted it so much, but I was afraid to say anything."

"I don' think I've ever been afraid of sayin' somethin' till now. What I might've said in the past wasn't important, but this is." He cupped her cheeks, staring deep into her eyes. "This is important, Scarlett. I want to see ya again. I don' want this to be the end."

"Yes." A smile broke free, and it felt like the sun appearing from behind the clouds, pouring warmth onto the Earth. "Yes, I want that too."

"So ya'll come see Scotland?"

"You couldn't keep me away."

He kissed her, long and hard, and when they got out of the bath, he made love to her. Every touch was a promise, an acknowledgment that this wasn't the last time they'd be together. They would see each other again, and when that time came, who knew?

Epilogue

FOUR MONTHS LATER

I t took four months to get to Scotland. Four months to save up the money, to finish her next project and get it off to her editor, to get her passport in order—because of course there was a freaking backup—but she didn't think those four months had been wasted. She'd spent them video chatting and talking on the phone with Gavin constantly. The man could talk for hours about nothing and she would still be entertained. And the more he talked about Scotland, the more she fell in love—with the man and the country. The only thing they disagreed about was him paying for her ticket to Edinburgh. Later, maybe, she would allow him to cover the cost, but for now she needed to pay her own way.

When she arrived at baggage claim at the airport in Edinburgh, Gavin was waiting. She stood out of the flow of traffic at the entryway and scanned the crowds for him, knowing he'd be there. His long strides ate up the distance before she even caught sight of him, and he swooped her off her feet, swinging her around in the air, his arms holding her so tight she could barely catch her breath. "I missed you, lass," he said, face buried in her neck.

They'd become her favorite words. Every time he said he missed her, his voice deepened and his eyes softened, and she could read the emotion there with her heart, not just her gaze.

"I missed you too."

Gavin kissed her neck, then her jaw, and then he was kissing her mouth until a woman passed by and mumbled something about getting a room. "What will the children think?"

"They'll think they love each other," the woman accompanying her said. Gavin eased back and laughed as he took Scarlett's hand, dragging her to the carousel to get her luggage.

She barely saw Edinburgh as they drove through. The city passed in a blur outside her windows, but she had eyes only for Gavin. Those curls still fell over his forehead, and his grin was still the slightest bit crooked, and his eyes were still the color of whisky. Stubble graced his cheeks. He hadn't changed a bit, and yet everything looked new; she soaked up the sight of him here, next to her, instead of on a screen a thousand miles away. He touched her constantly, his hand on her arm, fingers entwined with hers, hand on her thigh. She soaked it all in, unable to believe she was finally here, finally feeling his touch. It had been so long.

Guess it didn't matter if you were twenty-five or forty-five; the hunger to be together felt the same.

Gavin drove them outside the city, through what looked like suburbs. He'd been in an apartment when they first met, but the stay in Black Wolf's Bluff had inspired him, he said. He'd taken her along for the ride (virtually) as he explored the countryside to find a replacement. She hadn't seen the house he settled on, though.

"I want it to be a surprise. Ye're goin' to love it."

The homes grew more and more isolated until finally they pulled into a long, winding driveway. It disappeared between two hills up ahead, and when they passed between the hills and around a curve, the fields became woodland as far ahead of them as she could see. On a hilltop, barely poking above the trees, sat a house, and the minute they pulled up beside it, Scarlett knew he'd been right—she was in love with more than just Gavin.

"It's beautiful," she breathed, leaning forward in her seat to get a better view.

Pride beamed from Gavin's face. "I'm glad ya like it." The house was built from thick beams and stone, two stories, with massive windows staring down at them. She knew the windows on the opposite side were even bigger. Gavin had told her the back of the house looked out on a small loch, and she couldn't wait to see it.

He deposited her suitcase in his room, where the walls were a soft white with masculine navy-blue fabric at the windows and on the furniture. The room felt like him, and even better, it smelled like him. Sleeping surrounded by his scent was her idea of a dream. Sleeping with him beside her again would be magic.

They made dinner, ate, did dishes. All the things that seemed so mundane back home, but here, with Gavin, every moment meant so much. If she hadn't known before she came here that she was in love, she would've known the minute she saw him at the airport. But it was spending these moments of nothing special that convinced her. Only love could make washing the dishes delightful.

And yet, as long as they'd been talking, neither one of them had said it.

After dinner, Gavin took her out onto the back porch, which traveled the length of the house. At one end hung a swing much like the ones on the front porches in her town, though this one was piled with blankets and cushions. The air was chilly, the spring season cooler here than it was back in Tennessee. Gavin arranged the blankets, sat with a pillow behind his back, long-ways on the swing, then patted the seat between his thighs. "Come 'ere."

Resting back against him, she felt her heart melt when he wrapped his arms around her just as he had so often when he was in Black Wolf's Bluff. With blankets covering them for warmth, they sat in the silence and stared out at one of the most beautiful scenes she'd ever seen. The water of the loch was about thirty yards away, dark now that the sun had set, the reflection of the moon silver as it rippled across the water. The night was alive with the sounds of animals, though she couldn't identify most of them. The trees were the same— pine she knew, and the birch trees whose leaves reflected the silver light of the moon were easily identified. One grand oak stood to the left side of the wide backyard. Other than that, she would need Gavin to teach her about the flora as well as the fauna.

"You were right," she said as the swing gently rocked beneath them.

"About what?"

"About the air. It is different, just like you said. Soft. You can almost feel it, which seems weird to say, but it's true." She glanced up at him over her shoulder, taking in his handsome features from a new angle, admiring the hard lines and soft curves, everything that made Gavin, Gavin. "I love it."

He smiled, and she thought she detected a hint of relief. "I hoped you would."

She went back to watching the water, feeling Gavin's heart thump behind her, matching the rhythm of her breathing to his almost by instinct. Contentment relaxed her muscles, slowed her thoughts. She was almost drifting off when Gavin cleared his throat.

"I planned to wait till ya'd been here a few days, gotten used to the place, used to me," he said. His lips brushed her temple. "But I can't wait, Scarlett. I love ya. Ya know that by now, don' ya?"

Tears gathered in her eyes. "I didn't know, but I hoped."

A shudder went through him—relief? "Does that mean ya love me too?"

Her voice refused to work, so she simply nodded.

Gavin shifted behind her. His hands went to her hips, and then he was lifting her onto his lap, turning her to the side so she could see him. "Tell me," he demanded.

She smiled. "I love you, Gavin. I love you." Raising her hand to pet his cheek, feel the stubble on his face, she stared hard into his eyes, willing him to see the truth staring back at him. "You asked me once about adventures, but as much as coming here is an adventure, it doesn't compare to loving you. That's the biggest adventure of my life, but I'm ready for it. Ready for you."

Gavin kissed her then, hard and hungry, his mouth open, tongue demanding. She let him in, wanting everything he had to give. There was a lot still to decide, but the most important peace had fallen into place—their hearts. She'd never dreamed that flashing a Scotsman would end up this way, with the love of her life. But it had, and now that Scotsman was hers, for always.

Did you enjoy *40 AND FLASHING (THE SCOTSMAN)*? If so, please consider leaving a review at your favorite retailer to tell other readers about the book. And thank you!

For the latest on the next *SILVER FOXES OF BLACK WOLF'S*

BLUFF release (and yes, there will be more!), be sure to sign up for my newsletter at ellasheridanauthor.com.

Before you go…

Are you interested in reading the book Gavin read? That part of this story is based on the first book in my Assassins series. Take a look to see if you, like Gavin, can't get enough!

ASSASSIN'S MARK

I KNEW the minute I saw him that Levi Agozi was too perfect to be real. I didn't care. He came to me, asked for me, and, dazzled by his dark good looks and the bad-boy aura surrounding him, I gave in. Willingly.

MY FATHER IS SET to become the next governor of Georgia, and he'll use me to get there if he has to. He'll hand me over, virginity and all, to the man with the biggest bank account and political pull.

I WANTED SOMETHING MORE.

• • •

I WANTED LEVI. And I had him—until I woke up, drugged and confused, at his mercy. He's a bad boy, all right. A sexy, deadly assassin. And I'm the pawn torn between him and my father, two powerful men intent on destroying each other.

I MIGHT NOT UNDERSTAND their war, but I do understand one thing: no matter who wins, I lose.

Turn the page to read Chapter One of ASSASSIN'S MARK.

Chapter One

ASSASSIN'S MARK

I'm not sure what I expected. I'd been to bars, but not the kind of bars with pool tables and smoke haze and men on the prowl for a one-night stand. The bars I'd been to specialized in cocktail hours and old men in business suits. The Full Moon wasn't refined or elegant or quiet.

It was everything I was not. Exactly where I needed to be tonight.

"What'll you have?" the bartender asked. He was staring at Candy's breasts, but she didn't seem to mind, just flashed him a sexier version of her friendly smile. Had she slept with him before?

It was Renee who answered. "Pitcher of strawberry margaritas, Dave."

"Make that two," Candy tacked on.

Dave the Bartender nodded at her cleavage. "I'll send 'em right over."

I followed my friends through the crowd toward a table Sarah had snagged while we ordered. The three women obviously had a routine. I'd known they were close, and the fact that they'd extended their little circle to include me from the first day we met in Nursing 101 class had touched me in ways they couldn't possibly understand. They were normal girls with normal lives and normal homes. I wasn't, but if they'd noticed, they didn't mention it. No flicker of recognition at my name, no questions about where I lived or why I never went out when they invited me. Just basic friendship, no strings attached.

They had no idea how rare that was.

"So, Abby, see anything interesting?"

Too much, actually. Heat flushed my cheeks. "Um…"

Sarah giggled. "Wait till she's got at least one margarita in her, Renee. Then ask." She bumped my shoulder with hers. "The selection always looks better the later it gets."

The selection already looked pretty good to me. Most of the men were our age—early twenties—and not a suit and tie to be found. Jeans and half-buttoned shirts and messily styled hair were the go-to. A tattooed forearm or the wink of an earring wasn't rare. Beers in hand, the men joshed each other while prowling the room, hungry gazes assessing each woman they came to. One by one they'd peel off with their choice, either to the dance floor or a table or the front door.

What was it like to be the women they chose? In the circles my family required me to frequent, the barrier of my father's name and status kept men away from me. Here, there were no barriers except my friends and my own insecurities. The idea that I could choose to ignore both and do whatever I wanted quickened my breath. Either I was excited or about to hyperventilate; I wasn't certain which.

I refused to let the terror win anymore.

The margaritas arrived and we each poured ourselves one. The fruity yet tart liquid set my tongue alight like a sparkler on the Fourth of July, a pleasure I hadn't experienced before. I savored it as I listened to the girls' giggling commentary about each man who walked by. It wasn't long before the room went hazy with something other than smoke and I found myself joining in the conversation without reservation.

I was pouring my second margarita when my phone vibrated in my back pocket. Two shorts, one long: my father. A healthy gulp helped bolster my confidence before I pulled the cell out for a look.

I shouldn't respond, shouldn't care, but I clicked on the message anyway, just to see. Maybe he'd changed his mind. Maybe he was worried about me. Maybe he wanted to apologize, tell me he loved me for once in twenty-one years.

Where the hell are you?

Or maybe not. I returned the phone to my pocket.

Sarah leaned close, her voice low. "Everything okay?"

Renee and Candy were focused on the table of men to their right. I gave Sarah a wry smile. "My dad." I took another drink. "It'll blow over, I'm sure."

Sarah laid her hand over mine on the table and squeezed. The gesture mesmerized me. I couldn't remember the last time someone had touched me because they cared. How sad was that?

My phone buzzed again. I ignored it.

"Holy shit."

Sarah's hand left mine to grasp her drink. She took a gulp, her gaze trained somewhere over Candy's head. I followed it.

Holy shit is right.

The man was tall, dark, and dangerous with a capital *D*. I'd never seen anyone like him, anyone who made my insides clench just looking at him. Thick dark hair, long on top and shaved close on the sides, highlighted perfect ears and a jaw chiseled from granite. His eyes seemed too light for that hair and his olive skin, shining like spotlights beneath dark brows, almost too intense to bear. And those lips. *God.* They hinted at sensual pleasures I could only guess at.

He prowled across the room, a lean, muscular panther intent on prey—every woman's fantasy, including mine.

And he was headed straight for us.

My gaze dropped to my drink. The tables around us held either men or couples, so I wasn't mistaken about his focus. Which girl was he interested in? Sarah with her sweet smile? Or maybe Candy, with her unabashed sensuality?

An empty glass stared back at me. I reached for the pitcher.

"Hello, ladies."

My hand froze on the handle as the words quivered through my body. *Look up! Look at him!* But I couldn't; I could only sit there like a dumbass holding the pitcher in my shaking grip and praying I didn't make a fool of myself.

No fear, remember?

No fear. I tightened my grip, lifted. So far, so good. Somehow I managed to pour a fresh drink without spilling, replace the pitcher on the table. Despite the sick pounding of my heart in my throat, I made myself glance up.

Gray eyes locked with mine.

Lord, he's beautiful.

I expected him to look away, to focus on one of the other women. He didn't. He stared—at me. Until the urge to squirm crawled up my spine and my cheeks burst into flames.

"Hello."

Was that my voice, all breathy and…suggestive? It must've been; the other girls were staring, silent, their round eyes just as awed as I'm sure mine were. I looked back to the man looming over our table.

He reached a hand out to me. "I'm Levi."

My fingers settled into his grip like they had been created to fit him. "Abby."

My voice cracked. I cleared my throat.

"Hi, Abby." He didn't let go of my hand, didn't glance around. Just held me captive with those intense eyes. "Would you dance with me?"

Me?

I barely managed not to say it aloud. Instead I looked to Sarah, who was frantically nodding. "Uh, okay. Sure."

Could I be any more awkward if I tried? Where was the vaunted hostess who demurely handled every crisis that arose?

Maybe she'd died along with the dream that someday, somehow, my father would see me as his daughter and not his pawn.

Levi tugged on my hand, urging me to my feet. My body responded to his command automatically, breaking through the nerves that had held me frozen. I didn't want to be frozen, not anymore. And I didn't want to miss this, not a minute of it.

∾

Grab your copy of ASSASSIN'S MARK today!

About the Author

Born and raised in the Deep South, Ella Sheridan spent years telling herself stories before finally writing her own. Romantic suspense, paranormal romance, sexy contemporaries—she can't seem to stick to just one. Her goal in life is to finish every series she begins (if only she'd stop adding new series so that would be possible!).

Now Ella calls North Alabama home. Spending time cuddling with her two sweet tabbies, Oliver and Henry, is her number one priority, followed closely by writing, working, and writing some more (though she's recently found a little time to learn a new craft: watercolor painting). Connect with Ella at ellasheridanauthor.com or at the social media options below. For news on Ella's new releases, free book opportunities, and more, sign up for Ella's newsletter. Or join Ella's Escape Room on Facebook for daily fun, games, and first dibs on all the news!

www.ingramcontent.com/pod-product-compliance
Lightning Source LLC
Chambersburg PA
CBHW052008170626
46808CB00007B/2836